HARRIS COUNTY PUBLIC LIBRARY

W9-ASQ-820

YA   Blair
Blair, A. A.
Mystic of the midway : the letter /
$24.99   on1248897217

WITHDRAWN

Mystic of the Midway

A Crystal Beach Caper

A.A. Blair

Mystic of the Midway
The Letter

Histria Kids

Las Vegas ◊ Oxford ◊ Palm Beach

Published in the United States of America by
Histria Books, a division of Histria LLC
7181 N. Hualapai Way, Ste. 130-86
Las Vegas, NV 89166 USA
HistriaBooks.com

Histria Kids is an imprint of Histria Books. Titles
published under the imprints of Histria Books are
distributed worldwide.

All rights reserved. No part of this book may be
reprinted or reproduced or utilized in any form or by
any electronic, mechanical or other means, now known
or hereafter invented, including photocopying and
recording, or in any information storage or retrieval
system, without the permission in writing from the
Publisher.

Library of Congress Control Number: 2021937701

ISBN 978-1-59211-118-3 (hardcover)

Copyright © 2021 by Aaron Blair

Table of Contents

For Nathan, Miranda and Sarah

Foreword

Crystal Beach was a real amusement park in Fort Erie, Ontario, Canada. It operated for nearly 100 years, from 1890-1989. Much of Crystal Beach's history has been preserved by William E. Kae. His book, Crystal Beach Park: A Century of Screams, was a primary source of research for this story. The rides and attractions described in this book were all real. The characters and events are a work of fiction.

William E. Kae was wonderfully supportive throughout the creative process. He had donated a number of photos to the novel from his personal archive. Sadly, William E. Kae passed in September 2020 and as a result, was unable to see this book published. Mystic of the Midway is dedicated to his memory and his passion for the Crystal Beach Park.

Prologue: The Accident

Stephanie Rose Strawn, known as Effie by her friends, giggled as she raced across the school playground. She could hear the clumsy fumbling of her pursuer behind her. Effie ran with a light grace that enabled her to easily navigate obstacles. She raced up the climber stairs and crossed the wooden bridge. The bridge quivered under the light touch of her feet. Effie looked back to check the distance between herself and her pursuer. She was in no danger of being tagged.

Effie reached the highest level of the play structure. She could see the entire school from atop the platform. There were two possible exits, the slide, and the fireman's pole. The bridge was no longer an option as her pursuer slowly crossed it. The bridge bounced under his clumsy stomps. There was a ladder she could try but she would be trapped. The person chasing her could just go down the fireman's pole and beat her to the bottom. She could jump off the ladder midway, but the platform was pretty high. Hearing the huffing getting closer, Effie had to decide quickly. The slide was just as much a trap as the ladder. The hot plastic would squeal while pulling the bare skin of its victims, slowing their descent. It would have been just as bad as the ladder. Effie decided on the fireman's pole. She heard the bouncing of the bridge stop as her pursuer reached the platform. She had to act fast. Effie quickly leaped at the pole. As she felt the air beneath her, Effie turned to look back. She had escaped. As she sailed, she noticed the pole passing. She reached out to grab it. Effie was blinded from the gleam of the sun that reflected off the hot metal. The pole eluded her grasp and, in a moment, Effie plummeted to the ground.

Effie landed on her back with a hollow thump. The impact pushed all the air out of her. In fact, it pushed *her* out of herself. In a blink, Effie watched herself from what felt like above. She looked at her motionless body as children surrounded her, not knowing what to do. Floating, Effie tried to call out. No sound escaped her. Then what sounded like whispers swirled around her. They were voices, but she couldn't make out what they were saying. Effie felt enveloped by the whispers. They were clutching her, pulling her. Effie was scared. She wanted to escape, but she could not run. She floated helplessly as the whispers pulled her further from her limp body and concerned friends. The whispers tickled her ears. She felt them urging her to not struggle and follow them. But Effie was strong-willed. She focused all the energy she had and reached toward her body. The motion broke her free from the whispers' grasp and she felt herself soar away. Effie saw her body quickly approaching and with a slam was reunited with her flesh. Effie quickly sat up with a gasp that sucked in the surrounding air, filling her with life. The crowd around her leaped back in surprise. Effie heard some screams. She couldn't tell if they were joyful, relief or fear. But the surprise awoke the children from their inaction and they rushed towards her. Effie collapsed back to the ground. She was in a daze. The older children lifted her and carried her to the school nurse. Effie remembered hearing the children bark instructions at each other. Things quickly faded to black. She woke up in the hospital.

After the accident there was a lot of fuss by the school, her parents, the doctors and even her twin brother, James Gordon Strawn, whom everyone called Jimmy. At first, Effie didn't notice that things had changed for her. She had headaches and some dizziness. The biggest change for Effie were the whispers. The same whispers that she heard at the playground came back. They weren't always there and they didn't envelop her in the same way, but they were the same whispers. Effie would never forget them. The doctors who peered into her eyes and ears with mini flashlights said that these sorts of things might happen. Her parents were worried. *They* often whispered and looked at Effie with nervous eyes.

Thank goodness it was finally summer! Effie heard her parents say that she needed a 'break from it all,' but from what Effie could tell, they *all* needed a break.

Chapter 1
The Letter

Effie watched the countryside speed past: farm, field, farm, field, field, field, cows. The wind that rushed in from the open car windows whipped Effie's blonde hair into more of a mess than usual. It was a hot summer day, but the blowing air wasn't refreshing. It was just pushy, not to mention stale and hot! Effie heard the murmur of the radio but couldn't make out anything above the wind's howl. The windows were open because it was hot and their old car didn't have air conditioning; but the radio was definitely on for her. Effie liked to listen to *her* music loud. She knew her parents didn't. They were always telling her to turn her music down. But ever since the accident, it was her parents who listened to *their* music loud. Maybe listening wasn't the right word. The music was played so Effie and Jimmy *couldn't* listen. It was a trick her parents used so they could talk, but it really wasn't fooling anyone. Effie knew what they were talking about: her. Her parent's sideways glances told Effie she was the topic of conversation. As the family raced towards their cottage, it was as much to escape the city as to leave the bad memories, tests, doctor visits, and hospital stays all behind them.

Effie looked over at her brother. He was reading one of his detective novels, *Encyclopedia Brown and the...* missing something or other. Effie used to share everything with her brother. But after the accident, there became a wedge between them. Jimmy often hid behind a book, but Effie wondered if he was using the book to hide from her. Jimmy's sandy brown hair flickered from the wind just visible above the book cover that hid his face. Effie couldn't even think about reading in the car. She looked down at the bag in her hand. Since the accident, it didn't take long for Effie to be overwhelmed by motion sickness. The pale crumpled plastic stood out against the colorful quilt Effie and her brother sat on. It was meant to protect them from the hot plastic seats that could burn skin in the summer's heat. Even though Effie was told that all of her test results looked normal, which was the family's ticket to leave the city and go to their cottage, she knew the key word was *looked.* Effie knew she wasn't normal anymore. Especially not if *normal* meant she was supposed to feel exactly the way she used to feel before the accident. Since the accident, Effie often felt dizzy and sometimes she thought she heard or saw strange things. Things that weren't really there. Things that *couldn't* be there. No, Effie knew she wasn't normal, at least not anymore. But Effie also knew she wasn't broken. She wasn't some delicate vase that had to be handled with care. As she looked at Jimmy, Effie smiled. This cottage trip she was going to show her family, especially Jimmy, that she wasn't broken and hopefully dislodge the wedge stuck between them.

The car slowed down and Effie's hair rested on her head like a tangled nest. This was customary on this drive. The Strawns' cottage was in Crystal Beach, a beach town in Southern Ontario known for its amusement park. When they first started visiting Crystal Beach, Effie and her family used to sit in traffic jams that stretched as far as the neighboring town. The last few years, the wait had been much shorter. Effie could see the tips of the Giant rollercoaster and hear the screams as she saw the miniature cars zip over its hills. She could see the head of the Giant himself welcoming amusement park goers with his warm bearded smile.

The familiar sights and sounds of the park were interrupted with something new. Something Effie had never heard before. It started out as a rustling noise. Effie surveyed her family. The noise didn't seem to be coming from her family and they didn't seem to notice the sound either. As they approached the heart of Crystal Beach the noise got louder and changed into a familiar whisper. Her ears began to tickle. The whisper urged her to look out the window. That's when Effie noticed a young teenage girl. She was about the age of Effie's best friend in Crystal Beach, Lydia. Lydia was a few years older than Effie and her brother. But this girl's clothes made her look older. She wore a dress that looked as if it was from a different time. The girl was very pretty and Effie could see that she was staring at her. She had pale green eyes that sucked you in. And there was something more: she was soaked from head to toe. Sure, being wet came with beach town territory, but usually, it was accompanied by a bathing suit. Effie hadn't seen anyone go swimming in a dress so pretty, especially anyone older than four or five. She knew she wouldn't have wanted to ruin that sort of dress if it were hers. The material drooped from the weight of the water. The dress's playful polka dots looked like they were consumed by the dark navy-blue material. As Effie studied the stranger, the young girl broke their trance with a warm smile and a wave. Effie shook herself.

"Mom, Dad, do we know that girl?"

Jimmy pulled the book from his face and looked out Effie's window. Effie's mother did the same as her father checked the rear-view mirror.

"What girl, honey?" Effie's mother asked.

When Effie turned back, the girl was gone.

"I guess we missed her," Effie's father replied.

Effie grunted in agreement. Everyone resumed what they were doing. Jimmy read his book; her parents whispered beneath someone singing about answers blowing in the wind. And, like the song, the blow of the wind took the whispers and rustling sounds away.

Like many of the pastel-colored cottages that lined Maplewood Avenue, theirs was a small yellow bungalow. The cottage was at the center of Crystal Beach under a canopy of ancient trees where the mating calls of the cicadas drowned out the amusement park bustle. Effie's father, Michael, burst out from the chocolate-brown Dodge Dart.

"Alright gang, let's hit the beach!" Michael called.

Effie and Jimmy spilled out of the car. Effie's mother Elizabeth opened the car door. She had wild, untamable blond curls and sky-blue eyes like her daughter's. Elizabeth beamed; she loved coming back to her hometown. She gave a stretch so wide it was like she was giving all of Crystal Beach a giant hug.

"Such a beautiful day! I packed a bag, hon. You're all ready for the beach. I'll stay back to unpack and fix lunch."

Michael moved to the back of the car. The trunk was so large that when it swung open it blocked out the sun. The next sound was a familiar one: a loud gong from Michael's head as it banged against the trunk as if it were from that television game show her parents liked to watch. Effie thought her Dad should wear a helmet because he so often found creative ways of getting hurt. Whether it was getting his fingers caught in mousetraps or breaking his foot when showing children how to 'safely' operate a skateboard, Michael just had a knack. The wrong thing always happened at his expense. Despite this, he always remained in good spirits. During all of Effie's tests and uncertainty, her father stayed positive and met her fear with a warm smile. He knew she would be alright and because of that Effie believed it, too.

"Alright guys, we're off!"

Michael, Jimmy, and Effie made their way down Maplewood towards the beach. Michael was carrying two beach bags. His shoulders were piled high with towels. He resembled a pack camel being readied to cross the Sahara. Michael tried to balance the load with a beach umbrella under his arm. It was a disaster waiting to happen. Before Effie could offer to help, she remembered she had packed her sunglasses away and wanted them for the beach. They were like the ones she had seen Madonna wear in her music videos and she couldn't wait to show them to Lydia. Effie had already been on the lookout for her as they approached the beach.

"Dad, I forgot something."

Michael groaned and turned around.

"What are you missing, honey? Is it important?"

As Michael turned to talk to Effie, the inevitable happened. The umbrella hit a nearby tree. Effie could hear the uneven thump of things falling to the ground. Before Michael could begin to curse the tree for bumping into him, Effie took the opportunity to slip away.

"I'll be right back, Dad. I know where I left them"

Effie raced along Maplewood. The sunlight leaked through the canopy of trees along the street. Effie reached the cottage and opened the green-stained wood screen door. The cottage still had the musty smell from being closed all winter. Effie could hear an old love song coming from the kitchen. Effie saw her mother dancing with a piece of paper as if it were a person. She was smiling and gazing at it. Effie looked down and saw the bag where she had packed her sunglasses. She rummaged through it, found her sunglasses, and looked up.

From the front stoop where Effie stood, their two-bedroom cottage wasn't much. Effie's Dad always called it "cozy." Another word for really small. The only way to tell where one room finished and another room began was by the change in the floral wallpaper patterns and the brightly colored floor tile. Effie's mother was gone.

She must have gone back to unpack, Effie thought.

That was when Effie noticed the paper her mother had been looking at on the kitchen counter. The white of the paper stood out against the dark-tiled countertop.

She must have left it behind, Effie thought.

The paper seemed to almost glow. It quivered in the summer breeze calling to her. Listening to her curiosity, Effie made her way to the kitchen to take a peek. Effie's head began to throb as she approached the paper. The rustling sounds returned, tickling Effie's ear. Effie picked up the piece of paper. As she did, the whispers got louder, swirling around her. Effie could see there was writing on the paper but it was a blur. As the words came into focus, Effie realized it was some sort of letter.

The letter was written in cursive writing. She couldn't read cursive very well but she could tell it was a love letter. She could read the words *love, forever, happy,* and *kiss.* Her cheeks blushed. As her eyes scanned for more words, she looked at the bottom of the page. Effie felt her throat tighten. The name signed at the bottom wasn't her father's! Effie's mind raced. What could this mean? Her grip weakened and she felt the letter tug from her hand. It felt like the letter was being pulled away. Effie swooned. She lost her grip on the letter. It leaped from her hand and flew to her parents' room. Effie began to give chase but she heard her mother's voice singing to the music of another love song drifting out of the walnut-paneled stereo. She was coming back into the kitchen! Effie ran from the house. She didn't want to get caught. Effie knew what she did was wrong. She stole her mother's secret.

After getting a safe distance from the house, Effie stopped to catch her breath. Effie's head throbbed. With every breath Effie took, thoughts filled her head, like the air into her lungs. What did she just read? Was her mother actually in love with someone else? How could she do that to her father? Effie's memory began to fill the empty spaces. She had heard her parents talk about other children's parents divorcing. The stress of work, or money, or becoming different people – *whatever that meant.* Effie knew parents could fall out of love and separate. Then a realization hit her. What if it was because of her? What if *she* was the stress? What if her parents fell out of love because of all the doctor's appointments after the accident? Maybe the wedge she felt between her and Jimmy had also become a wedge between her mother and father? Effie rushed back to the beach but her father and Jimmy were gone. She was alone. The mating call of the cicadas became lonely. Their wail surrounded her, consumed her. She put on her neon sunglasses to hide the tears that were welling up in her eyes.

Chapter 2
Crystal Beach Friends

"Liz, you missed it. We had a perfect spot!!" Michael grinned, his teeth stained purple from too much loganberry soda.

Jimmy entered the cottage behind his father. His face was still buried in his book. Effie eyed him as he approached. He didn't look up. After she finally found her father and brother, Effie had been trying to get Jimmy's attention the whole time at the beach. It was impossible because their father had been *entertaining* Jimmy and Effie. Her father's attention made it hopeless for Effie to get some alone time with her brother to share her discovery and fears.

"Let's build a sandcastle!"

"Want to go get some wagon wheels? *Please*?!"

"Hey, do you think that guy over there will let us fly his kite?"

He did. That kite will never fly again.

Effie had enough. She needed to get her brother's attention. She shoved an elbow under Jimmy's ribs as he passed. Even the wedge couldn't protect him from Effie's sharp poke.

"Ouch! What's wrong with you?!"

Jimmy glared at Effie. Effie met his gaze. Her eyes widened and she raised her eyebrows in an *I have something important to tell you* kind of way. Jimmy understood immediately. The twins didn't need to say much to let the other one know when there was something important to discuss. Michael whipped around.

"Yeah Eff, what's wrong? You haven't been yourself. The whole time at the beach, *you* needed *my* full attention. Heck, you didn't even go in the water."

"I needed your attention?" Effie thought. She had wanted to take the attention *away* from her; she needed to be alone with Jimmy, to tell him the secret. She thought quickly.

"I think I'm still just a little carsick, Dad."

Effie's response satisfied Michael, who went from suspicious to sympathetic in a blink.

"Awww honey, let's get you some lunch. It'll help settle you."

Michael went into the kitchen. Elizabeth was at the olive-colored stove. She smiled and greeted Michael. Hearing her parents' whispers and her mother's giggle made Effie furious. How could her mother go on like that? It was one big lie! But the thought was stopped short when she felt Jimmy's elbow hit her ribs.

"Ow!"

Effie didn't need to ask why. She hadn't given Jimmy an answer to her glance. Before she could suggest they escape to their room, Elizabeth and Michael both turned to their children.

"Really guys, we're here for a couple of hours and you're already on each other's case?" Michael snapped

"They're just hungry. Lunch is ready. Come sit down to eat," Elizabeth sang. Elizabeth was a kindergarten teacher and was able to sustain a singsong approach despite any chaos around her. While all the doctors poked and prodded Effie, Elizabeth constantly tried to manage the mood with her singsong optimism. Effie knew the song was just a show. She could always hear her mother's frustration or fear behind her melodic words. Elizabeth poured fluorescent orange macaroni and cheese from a pot into brightly colored bowls sitting atop their lime green table.

Effie and Jimmy eyed each other as they sat down at the kitchen table. They knew they had to plan their getaway. Elizabeth placed the pasta-filled bowls in front of her family then sat down. The fresh bright-orange noodles steamed. The color was almost the same neon-orange as some of the plastic bangles Effie had brought from Toronto to give to Lydia.

As if on cue, there was a knock at the door. Michael groaned and flung his arms in the air. Effie and Jimmy were quick to seize their opportunity.

"We'll get it!" Jimmy and Effie said together.

They sprang to their feet and raced to the door.

It was Lydia Davies with her brother, Sniff, and their dog, Spinoza, who had been called Spinz ever since Jimmy and Effie had known the Davies. The Davies were their closest friends in Crystal Beach and Jimmy and Effie spent most of their summer with them. Lydia and Sniff lived in Crystal Beach year-round. Their father, Larry, owned a local sweet shop, which worked out well for Jimmy and Effie, but even more so for Michael and his sweet tooth. Effie had heard her parents refer to the Davies as 'high school sweethearts. They went to the same high school as Jimmy and Effie's mother. The families were tied together by history, old and new.

Lydia was thirteen. Effie loved having an older friend. Being from the big city gave Effie instant credibility with Lydia. In return, Lydia let Effie into her teenage world. Lydia wanted to know everything that was happening in the big city. What were people wearing? What were people listening to? Effie always brought Lydia a mixed tape with the latest music and usually some gifts. The gifts weren't large: pins of rock bands that she knew Lydia couldn't get, stickers, or packs of movie cards. This visit, Effie had brought Lydia neon-orange bangles. They became really popular the past year. The more you wore, the better.

Sniff, whose real name was Andrew, was Lydia's five-year-old brother. He had jet-black hair and gleaming blue eyes like his sister and father. Their skin was always tanned from the sun. The sun always made Lydia and Sniff freckle across the bridge of their noses. Sniff was the nickname his father gave him as a baby because his nose always seemed to be runny. Sniff and Lydia's father, Larry, always gave people nicknames.

Their dog, Spinz, was a shaggy mess of black, brown and white. He was small and no one knew what breed of dog he was. Spinz had one foggy grey eye, which was completely clouded over. Consistent with his mismatched fur, Spinz's other eye was bright amber. Because of his foggy eye, Spinz didn't have the best depth perception. He often bumped into things. Playing fetch with him was always an adventure. Lydia couldn't pronounce Spinoza when she was a toddler. Spinoza was shortened to Spinz, which was much more appropriate. When Spinz got excited, he would run in circles until he got so dizzy he couldn't walk straight.

"Good afternoon, Lydia and Andrew," Elizabeth sang as she came to the door. Effie could hear her mother's annoyance of having the family's lunch interrupted.

"Sniff!" Sniff corrected.

"Sorry, good afternoon, Sniff."

"Arrr, I'm a pirate!" Sniff replied.

Sniff had been wearing a pirate outfit since last summer — it wasn't really so much a pirate outfit but a t-shirt that had a pattern like a pirate outfit. Just in case there was any doubt what the shirt was supposed to be, it had letters printed across: *Pirate Captain: don't ARRRRRRRRRRRRgue.*

Sniff wore the shirt every day last summer and it looked as if the tradition would continue. Sniff started wearing the shirt when he decided that he would ride the Pirate and Jolly Roger at the amusement park. The problem was that he was too small to get on the rides last summer. Jimmy and Effie heard Sniff say, "they couldn't say no to a *real* pirate. Even if he *is* a *little* small."

Sniff still had the floppy cardboard sword he carried around from last summer. It drooped from being used too often. Sniff would use the sword to hit people, sometimes strangers, and could be heard threatening, "ARRRRRR! I'm going to make you walk the plank!"

There were times last summer when Sniff wore an eye patch but he kept bumping into things and falling down. After seeing Sniff collide with a number of things during a game of tag, his mother took it away.

"Can Jimmy and Effie come out to play?" Lydia asked.

"Sorry, hon, we're just sitting down to lunch" Elizabeth replied.

"ARRRRRRRRR I'm going to make you walk the plank!"

"Was that Pirate Sniff? Tell him when they come by for dinner tonight to be prepared for a duel," Michael called from the kitchen.

Sniff heard Michael's challenge and got excited. He started showing off his swordsmanship, complete with sound effects. Spinz started to run in circles. In one of Sniff's lunges, he tripped over Spinz and fell on his bum.

Effie interrupted. This was her chance. It was the escape she needed.

"But we can meet you at the park, after."

Lydia understood Effie's tone immediately: Effie needed to tell her something. Lydia picked Sniff up under her arm and made her way down the street. Spinz followed behind, walking in zig zags.

"Meet you there!" Lydia called back.

A wave of relief washed over Effie. Lydia had come just in time to rescue her from drowning in worry. She would be able to share her discovery and, more importantly, not feel alone.

Chapter 3
The Confession and the Bully

As Effie approached the park, she heard her brother call, "Wait for me!"

Effie was slender and ran effortlessly. Jimmy was stockier than his sister and, although he was fast in spurts, he struggled to keep pace.

The lonely park had a large multi-level blue and green play structure. The shiny metal slides gleamed in the hot Sun, blinding onlookers and warning potential park goers that they were hot to the touch. Aside from Lydia, Sniff, and Spinz, the park was empty, as usual. There were a few benches and a picnic table under a tree. The seating areas were littered with empty beer cans and cigarette butts, which indicated that the park did get used, even if it wasn't during daylight hours.

As Effie approached, she could see Spinz running at squirrels. Every time he started his chase, he missed badly. He was so far off that the squirrels weren't even running from him. They watched Spinz with curiosity as he crashed into nearby bushes.

"Lydia!"

Sniff was digging in the sandbox, completely focused and unaware of the world around him. He was muttering something about buried treasure.

As soon as Effie got close to Lydia, she burst into tears.

Jimmy and Lydia rushed to her side. They looked at each other, confused.

"My Mom has a love letter from someone else!" Effie cried.

"What?!?" Jimmy was more surprised than Lydia. Lydia said nothing; she just stared at the both of them.

"How do you know?" Jimmy asked sharply.

"She was reading it. She looked so happy. I didn't know! I just wanted to see what it said." Effie took a deep breath, trying to contain her tears.

"It wasn't from Dad!"

The friends stood in an awkward silence.

"Let me see it!" Jimmy demanded.

"I don't have it."

"Hmmmph, no evidence?" Jimmy huffed.

"I'm not lying!"

"Well, what did it say?" Lydia interrupted.

"It was in cursive, so I couldn't read it exactly," Effie replied between sobs.

"What?!?" Jimmy exclaimed.

"But I could tell it was a love letter. I know it wasn't Dad's handwriting and I know the signature wasn't Dad ...it started with an H — a Harry, or a Harley or something."

"Alright, so you found a letter that you couldn't read and have decided it means Mom and Dad are getting a divorce? Seriously Eff?"

"I told you, I'm not making it up!"

"We know you're not Effie, just, can you be sure?" Lydia said, trying to calm everyone down.

Jimmy threw his hands in the air. "I mean really Eff, every Sherlock Holmes novel I've ever read tells you – you need the eviden..."

"What's that bookworm?" a voice interrupted.

The three friends whipped around. Maurizio, was standing behind them. They hadn't noticed him approaching. Maurizio, or Mertz as he was called in the neighborhood, was a bully. He didn't like Jimmy and Effie. They were out-of-towners. Most of the time how Mertz felt didn't matter. He wouldn't "express his feelings" around adults, but there were no adults at the park.

"What's a book going to do now? It's not gonna save you or your cry-baby sister."

"Shut up, Mertz." Lydia snapped.

"How about you make me!" Mertz said defiantly. Mertz had dark hair and eyes. He was a year or two older than Jimmy and Effie but shorter. Effie figured this was why Mertz acted the way he did: he wanted people to think he was bigger. He wore tank tops of his favorite wrestling stars, like the Junkyard Dog, Macho Man Randy Savage, or Hulk Hogan. He'd flex his muscles trying to intimidate people like he *was* one of the wrestling stars.

"You're goin' down!"

"Oh, Yeah!"

"Watcha gonna do?"

These were some of Mertz's favorite sayings. Mertz didn't usually get this close to Jimmy. He bumped him.

"Watcha gonna do?" Mertz croaked in a voice like Hulk Hogan.

Jimmy was more concerned about Effie and her discovery than getting into a fight with Mertz. He shook his head and turned to Effie.

"I need to see that letter, Eff!"

"I don't have it!"

"What, are you chicken? Don't blame you? You want a piece of this? – Ouch!"

During Mertz's attempt to fight Jimmy, Sniff had finished burying whatever he was burying in the sand box and had made his way over to see what was going on. While Mertz was flexing, Sniff bit his leg.

"Arrrr, I'm going to make you walk the plank!"

Spinz got excited and began to bark and run in circles. Just then, Lydia noticed Mertz's older brother Eugene riding his bike. Eugene looked exactly like Mertz except, where Mertz wished he had muscles, Eugene had actual muscles, a lot of them. He was Lydia's age.

"Oh, Eugene! Why is your brother so annoying?" she called.

Eugene, who had been staring at Lydia, something he did regularly, called out, "Mertz! Get home before I whip your butt!"

Mertz wailed, "Awww Euge?"

"Get going!"

Mertz's shoulders drooped. He shot Sniff and Jimmy a mean look and began to walk home.

"Eff, we have to get evidence!"

"I told you, I'm not lying!"

"Still, we need to be sure, investigate, find out all the facts before we tell Dad."

Effie was silent. She hadn't thought about what was next. All Effie had wanted to do was to tell Jimmy and Lydia. She knew telling her father was something they *could* do, but it was the last thing she wanted to do. Effie fell silent. Lydia noticed the awkward pause.

"We're coming over tonight. Maybe we can get our parents to give us clues."

Effie and Jimmy nodded. They began to walk home. With a plan in mind, the friends' thoughts began to drift. The image of Eugene floated into Effie's mind. She looked at Lydia. She noticed 'something' when Lydia called to Eugene. Effie felt something. She was sure of it.

"Eugene is cute," Effie whispered to Lydia.

"He's okay, I guess." Lydia's face flushed a little and her eyes darted away. "Can you believe Sniff bit Mertz?" Lydia began to laugh, changing the subject.

Effie laughed, "He didn't see that coming. Sniff, why'd you bite him?"

Sniff shrugged. "He said you want a piece of me."

"I'm not sure that was the pirate way," Lydia giggled.

"Sure it is. Pirates fight dirty," Sniff replied in a matter-of-fact kind of way.

Chapter 4
The Investigation

The Davies were right on time for dinner.

"Liz! Where's that husband of yours? Not in the hospital already is he?"

Larry rustled Jimmy's hair with his large hairy hand as he walked in.

"Hey, Sherlock."

Larry wasn't much taller than Liz, but he was much larger. He had wide shoulders and large arms that he wrapped around Liz as she came out of the kitchen to greet them. His hands and arms were covered in hair. Actually, most of Larry was covered in hair: his arms, back, chest, and he had a big bushy black moustache with dark stubble around his face. The only part of Larry that didn't have any hair was the top of his head, which was shiny bald surrounded by a bushy, curly mane.

Jodi was shorter than Liz, but like Larry was to Michael, she was larger. She had dark hair but not the crystal blue eyes that the rest of her family had. Jodi always wore colorful jewelry and often talked about the power of crystals. Effie loved listening to her. Jodi seemed like the only adult that believed in the world of magic the way kids do. She hugged Liz with one arm. In her other arm, she held a plate covered in tinfoil. She placed it on the kitchen table and held both of Liz's hands.

"You look so fresh, Liz! Your aura is so happy! What are you planning?"

Liz flushed and hugged her friend.

Michael came in from the backyard barbeque with a plate full of steaming charred meat. Larry grabbed the plate.

"Let me get that for you, fella!"

Once the plate was a safe distance from Michael, Larry greeted Michael with a hearty clap on the back.

Liz put out serving plates filled with gooey red pasta and steamed vegetables that glistened from their buttery coating. She started to hand out plastic plates to the kids and formal plates to the adults.

"Here you go. Help yourself. Eat out back. There's enough of a mess to clean in the house already."

As the adults piled their plates high with food, Lydia, Jimmy, and Effie took the opportunity to slip away.

"We'll be right there, Mom! I just wanted to show Lydia something I brought from home."

"Okay, come and join us in the backyard after," Liz called back.

Jimmy pulled Effie and Lydia into the twins' bedroom and closed the door.

"Okay, where is the letter?" Jimmy asked Effie.

"I don't know. It was in the kitchen when I saw it." Effie remembered the letter's flight into her parents' bedroom.

"I think it's in their bedroom."

"Effie, you go in and look for it. Lydia and I will stand watch."

"Me?"

"You're the only one who knows what it looks like."

Lydia nodded.

"Okay," Effie reluctantly agreed.

After the adults had left for the backyard, the friends crept out. Lydia took position just outside the bedroom. Jimmy went in the kitchen pretending he was getting his food ready. Sniff was nowhere to be seen. He was too young to be trusted with the secrecy of their mission.

Effie began looking around her parents' bedroom. The deep green wallpaper made the room especially dark. The green, along with the teak-colored furniture, made Effie feel like she was deep in a forest. Her heart was thumping. She was finding it hard to concentrate. She looked around but couldn't see where her mother could have put the letter. She looked on top of bedside tables and dressers. On the bed, there was a thick pile of duvet covers for the cool summer nights of early July. Effie began pulling drawers open. She looked quickly. The pounding in Effie's heart moved to her head. She froze when she thought she heard a noise. At first she thought it was coming from inside the bedroom. Was it the same sort of rustle she had heard earlier? It seemed to come from behind the wall. Effie's head started to throb. The noise couldn't be coming from inside the room.

Was it outside of the bedroom?

Was it steps?

Was it Jimmy coughing?

Was Lydia saying something?

Effie's head pounded. She couldn't be sure so she kept looking. Effie noticed the tall dresser. She couldn't see what was on top. Effie climbed over the bed, sinking into the brown striped duvet covers. She tried to move closer to the dresser. She felt like the duvet covers were slowing her down like quicksand. She couldn't quite see everything on top.

Wait. Was Lydia making more noise?

Jimmy was definitely saying something.

What was that the sign someone was coming?

Effie was starting to panic: *Wait, we didn't decide on a sign!*

Thoughts raced through Effie's head. She felt lost and alone in the dark forest of her parents' room. She heard a scramble outside the bedroom. Jimmy was stomping around and talking loudly. Lydia was suddenly stricken by a coughing fit. She knew they were trying to warn her. Effie looked around for a place to hide. There were no closets or curtains to hide within. Her heart raced. Effie felt like it was going to burst. What was she going to say?

Effie's head throbbed. She was getting dizzy as the rustling noise got louder. It began to consume her. Effie could no longer tell if the scramble was coming from outside or inside her parent's bedroom. Effie looked around. There was definitely noise coming from inside the room. As she tried to find the source of the noise she noticed a glow from behind the wall. The walls seemed to breath behind the glow, pulsating out towards her. Effie froze in fear. Was this really happening? Then Effie heard the door knob twist. The room became silent and Effie was trapped! Effie looked at the pile of duvet covers. She wanted to crawl under them and hide. Actually, it was the only option! She pulled the duvet covers up.

"AAAAAAAAAAAAAAAAARRRRRRRRRRR, are you trying to steal my buried treasure?"

Sniff leapt out, floppy sword in hand. Effie was so surprised she let out a scream. Liz entered the room.

"What's going on in here? Why is everyone acting so strange?" She looked back at Jimmy and Lydia, who crowded behind her, trying to peer into the bedroom. They both wore worried expressions.

Effie thought quickly.

"Sorry, Mom we were just looking for Sniff. He was hiding in here."

Effie collected Sniff, who was struggling to free himself.

"You won't get me to walk the plank!"

Liz sighed.

"Andrew!"

"SNIFF!"

"Sniff, come join us for dinner. We miss our fearless captain."

Sniff freed himself from Effie and straightened up as if he *was* a pirate captain. He walked out the room, "I'm going to eat me grub with me hands!" Sniff said in a dignified manner.

Liz shook her head.

"Thanks, Mom." Effie's voice shook. She never lied to her mother. Liz looked at Effie and smiled.

"C'mon hon."

Effie walked out of the bedroom. Jimmy and Lydia stared at her. Their eyes both spoke: *Well, did you find it?*

Effie shook her head. Lydia and Jimmy's shoulders sunk. They collected their food and joined the adults out back. Effie couldn't focus. She was swimming in her own thoughts. She heard the adults talking about adult things.

"So, is this new guy going to turn things around?"

"Said he's going to bring back the boats. I think that's the key."

"Finally investing some money in the place. More than just a fresh coat of paint I hope."

"Can't put lipstick on a pig and say it's something other than a pig."

These were the things the adults talked about. They didn't mean much to Effie. The friends couldn't talk about their failed plan. They just sat and listened. When dinner was done, the adults built a fire and Larry unveiled the treats. Different jellies, chocolate and maple were handed out. Michael's eyes danced more than the flames from the fire. Liz fetched her guitar and began to sing folk songs that were nothing like the music Effie listened to on the radio. To Effie, her mother's songs were happy and familiar and filled with hope.

Larry handed out multi-colored marshmallows for roasting. Jimmy and Sniff collected sticks. The friends sat in silence. The stars were out, lighting the night sky. Sniff roasted his marshmallows until they caught fire and then proceeded to slice the air to put out the flame. He made sound effects, pretending he was a pirate swordsman. The light trailed behind Sniff's slices, creating streaks of light in the air. Effie sighed. The smell of the fire and marshmallows tickled Effie's nose with their sticky sweetness. Her worry began to melt away. She was still confused about everything that had happened. But these were the moments she loved about her time at the cottage. They were familiar. Friends Effie had known whose parents had divorced always confided that things changed. Home became *unfamiliar*. Could her parents really be in trouble if they could still share these moments? The familiarity made Effie feel safe. Effie even began to sing along to some of the words she knew, something about a yellow taxi and paradise.

Chapter 5
The First Dream

Effie tossed in her sleep. She dreamt she was at the amusement park. It was busier than usual and Effie noticed that everyone was oddly dressed. The kids wore jeans with colorful patches, tie-dye shirts and had long scruffy hair. The adults all seemed very formal. The men wore short-sleeved collared shirts and dress slacks. Their hair all looked the same: cut short, almost as if they were in the army. The women wore pastel-colored blouses and knee-length skirts. The adults looked as if they were on their way to church, not spending an afternoon at an amusement park.

As Effie observed the crowd through the hot haze, she noticed someone staring at her: a thin boy with a wisp of light-colored hair above his lip. He stood in a game booth. Unlike the other game operators, he didn't taunt the passers-by. His hair was bright brown, almost a blend of blonde, brown and red. It was curly and looked as if it exploded from his head. He wore a uniform: bright red striped shirt and navy pants. He had a smattering of pimples and wore metal-rimmed glasses. Effie couldn't say he was handsome, but there was a confidence about him that she felt drawn to. He smiled as he approached her. He offered her a chance at a game. Effie could feel her face flush. She looked for money but realized her navy polka-dot dress didn't have any pockets. Effie paused. She didn't own a dress like the one she was wearing. But it looked oddly familiar. Effie felt the folds of the soft material quiver in the wind and dance when she moved. She was about to say that she didn't have any money when the boy handed her some rings. And winked.

Effie tried her luck at tossing a ring on a bottle for a prize. She did horribly but, for some reason, she didn't care. The boy laughed and gave her prizes every time anyhow. Effie could feel herself laugh and a warm feeling growing in her chest that spread to her fingertips. She ended up with a large stuffed bear. She couldn't contain her delight.

"What should I name him?"

"How about you name him after me?" the boy responded.

"But I don't know your name."

"It's Har…"

Effie awoke to the clatter of her father.

"Gotta get up! Want to beat the cars!" Her father clamored, stirring everyone from their sleep.

Chapter 6
The Amusement Park

Sniff and Lydia joined the Strawns on their trip to the park. Effie loved the park in the morning. Without the crowds around, there was a rhythm to the swoosh of the water rides and rumble of the Comet and the Giant coasters.

Effie was in happy spirits after her dream. She didn't mind waiting in the line to enter the park despite her father's grumbles of the unwelcomed change to park's entrance fee policy. But Effie enjoyed looking at the park in motion as they waited. Effie loved watching people. But this time the wait was different. The buildings looked different than how she remembered. They weren't as colorful. They were fresh and clean but Effie thought they didn't look as 'happy' as they used to. The Magic Palace just wasn't as magical. As soon as they entered the park, Sniff began to pull Lydia's arm.

"Let's go to the Jolly Roger!"

"What's the rush, Sniff? We have all day," said Michael.

"Arrrr, I don't want to spend one minute in this baby place. It's no place for a pirate!"

Michael laughed aloud.

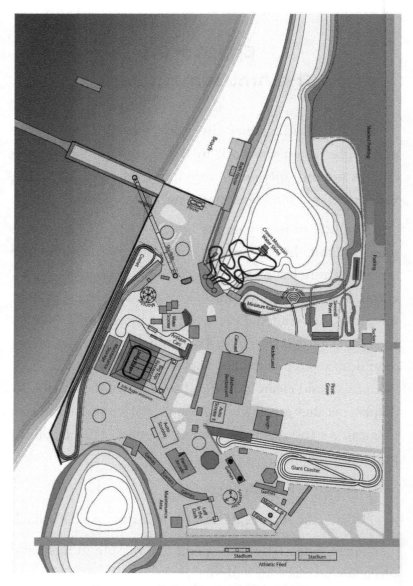

Layout of the Park (1981-1983)
Photo: Wliiam E. Kae

"Alright, as long as you stay with Lydia, you guys can run ahead!"

"Yes!" Sniff exclaimed. "You're my first mate!" He appointed Michael. Sniff tried to run and nearly pulled Lydia down.

"Sniff! Don't worry. We're going. You're not going to turn into a baby if we walk!"

Sniff stopped pulling, but he started to walk ahead. As they passed the games areas, they heard the catcalls from the game operators trying to lure park goers into a play. Effie found herself looking for the boy she had dreamed about. The uniforms were much different: simple t-shirts and dark jeans. The boy from her dream definitely wasn't part of the current amusement park staff. Michael, who loved a challenge, started to talk back to one of the game operators. He stopped and began negotiating the rules.

"We'll meet you at the Merry-Go-Round! I'm going to win your Mom a prize!" Michael said confidently. Elizabeth giggled. Effie's teeth clenched.

Jimmy whispered in Effie's ear, "We need to keep an eye on them!"

Effie nodded. She looked back. Her father was animated, gesturing to the game operator. Her mother had her arm around her father. Effie didn't understand. They looked happy. Effie couldn't understand how her mother could seem so comfortable with her father but get love letters from someone else. Effie felt her face flush. The thought of her mother hurting her father made her angry. But what she saw just confused her anger. She didn't know what to think or how to feel.

As they passed the rides and arcades, Effie heard the familiar rustling noise. It started as a tickle, pulling Effie's attention towards a corner of the park. Effie shifted her view towards the noise. It seemed to come from the Laff in the Dark ride. Effie could see the ride's bright red exterior. Effie shuddered. The Laff in the Dark ride had always creeped her out when she was younger. The effects of the ride didn't scare Effie. It was the slow walk to get on the ride. Something about the animatronic figures that stared out behind glass. What creeped Effie out most were the two smiling plastic faces of Laffin' Sam and Sal. Their broad smiles seemed menacing, threatening potential ride goers. Effie always felt that their shiny eyes always stared at her.

Effie felt a sharp yank on her arm. The whispers that fluttered around her head scattered into the air.

"Where are you going? This way!"

Effie looked at Jimmy's hand holding her arm and looked in the direction she was headed: straight towards the Laff in the Dark. Effie followed Jimmy's lead. They had lost

Park Entrance
Photo: Sue and Rudy Bonifacio

Jolly Roger
Photo Sue and Rudy Bonifacio

their parents. Jimmy huffed. He looked at Effie with blame in his eyes.

"C'mon, let's find them," Jimmy said, leading Effie with his hand still locked around her arm.

Jimmy and Effie found Sniff with arms crossed, standing outside the Jolly Roger. It was closed and Sniff wasn't impressed. The teenager who was standing guard explained that the ride was closed for maintenance.

"Don't worry little guy. It will be open soon." The teen's face was red from the sun and pimples.

"I still think he should walk the plank!" Sniff huffed to Lydia.

Jimmy shuffled. He didn't want to linger.

"I'll be at the Penny Arcade!" Jimmy informed the group.

As Jimmy faded into the crowd, Effie spotted the green-eyed girl. She was wearing the same dress and was still soaked from head to toe. She smiled and waved at Effie. Effie looked around. She was alone. Sniff and Lydia had moved on and Jimmy was gone. The girl waved her over. Effie began towards her. As Effie approached, the girl darted away. Effie ran after her. She didn't want to lose sight of her again. Effie felt the girl had something important to tell her. As she closed in on the girl, Effie saw her enter the Magic Palace. Before entering, she turned and smiled at Effie, giving her another wave.

Effie rushed into the entrance of the palace only to find herself immersed in darkness. She felt along the walls hoping that she was still following the girl. The hall opened into a room and a flood of light surprised and blinded Effie. As her eyes focused, she found herself standing in a room with a window. Light came from behind the glass, revealing a smiling flower girl sitting on a cushion. The girl was dressed like the hippies Effie had seen in her parents' old photo albums. As the cushion rotated, Effie saw a horrible ogre staring back at her. Although it wasn't the first time Effie had seen the effect, it startled her more than usual. She sighed.

I must have lost her

Effie thought to herself. If the girl had gone through the ride, the effect would have been triggered and Effie would have seen light when she approached. No, she had to be the first to trigger the flower girl. Effie was about to turn back when she heard a girl's playful laugh ahead. There was something odd about the laugh. Effie somehow knew the strange girl was its owner. Effie had to follow, had to find her. She was plunged back into darkness. When she emerged, she found herself in the middle of an obstacle course. The ground was covered in water. She had to hop on lily pads to cross the room without getting her feet wet. Effie stopped. She was alone. Water slightly covered the lily pads, making it impossible to get through without wet feet. Effie imagined it couldn't have always been that way. She dipped her toes in, creating a ripple. The girl couldn't have come this way either. The water was too still. Effie looked behind the rippling water at her reflection. Effie felt her chest tighten. The reflection in the water wasn't her! It was the mystery girl! Effie's heart began to race. She heard a scream behind her. It wasn't a scream that someone would usually hear in an amusement park. It had a different quality.

Effie was reminded of a time when her mother screamed at her after she ran from their car into traffic. Effie remembered feeling a car whiz by her face. She still remembered how close the car was to her. It was so close that Effie remembered feeling the heat from the metal door rush past her. This scream had that same quality. It made the hair on the back of her neck stand up.

Effie turned to find she was alone. Looking back into the water she saw her own panicked reflection staring back at her. She was afraid. Effie felt as if the walls were closing in on her. She rushed out of the room. Her feet splashed through the wet floor, missing every lily pad along the way. Effie rushed back the way she had come and plunged back into the darkness. She closed her eyes through the 'flower girl exhibit', afraid of what she'd see. Effie emerged at the ride's entrance relieved to feel the warm sun on her face. She grabbed the railing of the stairs and braced herself. She tried to catch her breath but her lungs were tight. It was as if she were drowning in fear.

"Effie?"

Effie looked up to see Lydia walking with Sniff. Tears had been streaming down his face.

"Effie, are you alright?"

Effie didn't know what to say. She was definitely *not* all right. She wasn't sure what was real. All Effie could do was nod.

"Just running too much." She gasped.

"Where's Jimmy?"

"Penny Arcade."

Effie found enough strength in her legs to move forward and join her friends.

Lydia told Effie that Sniff's luck didn't get better. He was too small to ride the Pirate and his appeal that he *was* a pirate didn't compel the ride operator to make an exception. The friends met Jimmy at the Penny Arcade. Jimmy was trying to look casual as he watched his parents.

"Where were you?" Jimmy asked Effie in a loud whisper. Effie couldn't tell Jimmy what had happened. She wouldn't be able to explain it. Effie only managed a shrug.

"Anything yet?" she asked.

Jimmy shook his head; his eyes were off in the distance. Effie followed his gaze to see her mother and father walking together. Liz was hardly visible behind a huge Pac-Man toy.

Lydia was trying to console Sniff.

"Whatcha gonna do?" Mertz's voice interrupted. Mertz emerged from behind one of the games and stood in front of the friends. He was standing close to Jimmy, trying to stare him down. Jimmy was more interested in his parents. But when he looked up from Mertz, his parents were gone. Jimmy searched the crowd for his parents. Effie also noticed and looked into the crowd. They had lost their parents.

"Who you lookin' for? There's no one that's gonna save you from me." Mertz hissed.

The mixture of Mertz's taunts, the noise of the Penny Arcade and amusement park chatter started to melt together for Effie. It became a jumbled murmur. Effie felt a whisper tickle her ear.

"The pier," the whisper called.

Effie looked towards the pier and saw her mother sneaking off on her own, trying her best to be inconspicuous.

Arcade
Photo: Rudy Wolowiec

Magic Palace
Photo: William E. Kae

"C'mon bookworm. You're gonna feel the wrath of these pythons!" Mertz started to flex his arms.

Effie noticed that Jimmy had seen their mother, too. Annoyed that Jimmy wasn't paying attention to his taunts Mertz pushed Jimmy and yelled, "Are you gonna fight?"

Jimmy immediately broke into a run.

"Where are you going, you chicken?"

Lydia immediately got into Mertz's face. "What's wrong with you, Mertz?"

Effie began to run after her brother.

"I ain't got no problem with you, Lidz," Mertz protested.

"Arrrr, I'm going to make you walk the plank!"

"Ouch!"

Effie couldn't see why Mertz called out in pain, but she could guess. Effie chased after her brother. She couldn't see him any longer. Effie ran towards the pier, where the whispers had told her. As she ran, her head swiveled from side to side, scanning for her brother or mother. The further she ran into the heart of the park, the more crowded it was. Effie passed the restaurants, Merry-Go-Round, Flying Bobs, and Tilt-A-Whirl. She was almost at the pier but couldn't find them through the thick crowds. Then Effie saw a lone person facing the opposite direction of the other park goers. It was Jimmy. He was staring intently into the distance. Effie scrambled to see what Jimmy was looking at. She saw her mother talking to a man. Effie had never seen the man before, but there was something oddly familiar about him. He was thin, wore glasses, and had a slight mustache. His hair was shaggy light-brown. Although he looked like Effie's mother's age, his curly hair seemed to make him more youthful. Effie had never seen her mother look so nervous. Liz spoke quickly; her eyes darted around anxiously. It was obvious that she didn't want to be seen. Effie hadn't realized that she had stopped completely still. She was in shock. Someone bumped her.

"Hey, watch it!"

Lydia ran to her side with Sniff following behind. Lydia grabbed her arm.

"Effie! You all right? Watch where you're going jerk!" Lydia snapped at a teenager wearing a cut-off shirt with a neon-pink *RELAX* printed on the front. The teen casually pointed to the printed letters in response to Lydia. He didn't use his pointing fingers.

Lydia turned to face Effie and noticed where Effie was looking. She saw Liz rushing off.

"What happened?"

Effie began to cry. "She was talking to a man. Someone I've never seen!"

Jimmy joined them.

"C'mon guys, let's go."

The friends followed. Lydia put her arm around Effie. They walked in silence. Jimmy was muttering to himself, something about 'evidence.' They found Michael by himself. He was struggling to eat a large sugar-covered wagon wheel while balancing a bottle of loganberry soda and holding the giant stuffed Pac-Man he had won.

"Hi, guys!" Michael called, noticing the children approach.

"I don't know what this is, but it's the biggest prize they had!" Michael said, referring to the stuffed Pac-Man.

"I won it for your mother!" Michael said proudly. As he got excited, Michael bumped into a young park-goer knocking over his food and drink. "Oops! Sorry!"

Michael stopped. He noticed Effie had been crying. "Honey, what's wrong?"

"She got hurt on one of the rides. We bumped heads," Jimmy quickly explained.

"Oh Honey, are you going to be okay?" Michael asked, dropping the Pac-Man. He went to check on Effie.

"How many fingers am I holding up?" Michael said, flashing a series of fingers in front of Effie. This was one of the standard tricks he used in the hospital. Effie could see past her father's smile to the familiar worry in his eyes.

"Can we just go home?" Effie asked.

Michael looked around at the kids, unsure. Liz arrived out of breath and flushed.

"What's going on?" she asked with a concerned look at Effie.

"Effie got hurt. She wants to go home. Where've you been?"

"The washroom" Liz lied.

Effie could see her father exchange a look with her mother. It was *the* look. The look her parents shared after the doctor's visits, tests, and every answer Effie gave during her recovery. It always annoyed Effie, but today it made her mad.

"Oh Hon, are you sure? How about we rest and see if you feel..."

"I want to go home!" Effie snapped at her mother.

Michael and Liz jumped in surprise.

"I think we all want to go home, Mom." Jimmy interrupted. After a pause, Lydia and Sniff nodded.

"This place is for babies, not a pirate!" Sniff huffed.

Michael and Liz looked at each other.

"If you guys are *sure...*" Michael paused, hoping the kids would change their minds. They all nodded in unison. Michael shrugged, picked up the giant stuffed Pac-Man, and began to walk to the exit. Liz took her prize from Michael, knowing that it, and everyone around them, were safer If she held on to it. The family walked out of the park in silence.

Chapter 7
The Second Dream

Effie had another restless night. She found herself dreaming about the amusement park again. In her dream, Effie stood in line at the Laff in the Dark ride. It was nighttime, and there were lights that were strung throughout the midway, giving it a festive look.

She felt a hand close on her shoulder. Effie quickly turned to find the boy who had let her win at ring toss.

"Boo!" he said with a playful smile.

Effie found herself smiling back. She liked this boy and felt she knew him more than just from playing a carnival game.

She looked back at the ride.

"Do we have to go in? This ride always gives me the creeps."

The boy laughed.

"There's nothing to be afraid of. Anyway, you have me. If you get scared, just hold me close."

Effie suspected this was the boy's plan all along. She looked up at Charmin' Charles, the piano-playing skeleton

Laff in the Dark
Photo: William E. Kae

who welcomed Laff in the Dark riders. She shuddered at his hollow eyes. Effie felt a chill run up her back as the beaming plastic faces of Laffin' Sam and Sal watched them pass by. Their glossy eyes glittered in Effie's direction. Effie watched them intently, almost expecting them to speak.

"Don't worry. Like I said, I'm right here."

Effie felt the boy tug at her arm. The Laff in the Dark car was in front of her. She looked at his warm smile. She didn't know why, but she trusted him.

The ride started with a jerk, and then they were plunged into darkness. Effie knew the ride well. It made sharp turns in the dark then would surprise you with scary images or figures. But this time, when the lights went on, Effie saw something she didn't expect.

At the first stop, the light revealed her parents. They were crying and sad. Effie was confused. She looked at the boy who was smiling and laughing.

"See, nothing to worry about."

The next was Jimmy and Lydia. They were dressed in black and holding flowers. Like her parents before, they wore sad expressions.

"What's going on?" Effie asked.

But the boy was gone. She was alone. Water started to rush into the car. Effie knew she had to get out but something stopped her from moving. Effie looked down to see chubby plastic hands holding her in place. She looked up to see Laffin' Sal and Sam on either side of her. They still wore their plastic smiles and ridiculous clothing. They stared at her.

"Where are you going dearie?" Sal asked.

"I have to get out of here!" Effie panicked.

"You can't leave. This is your destiny," Sam laughed.

"You can never escape your destiny," Sal agreed.

Effie tried to scream, but the water that had now completely covered the car rushed into her mouth and began filling her lungs. Effie struggled but could not escape from under the firm hands of Laffin' Sal and Sam.

Chapter 8
"Babysitting" and the Photo

Effie woke up coughing and gasping for air. Her heart raced from her dream. The sun peeked through the plastic blinds. It created a cage-like effect against the blue and white nautical-themed wallpaper. Effie usually found the wallpaper pattern soothing. She didn't feel that way after her nightmare. Effie felt like she was in the middle of a storm; her life like the unstable waters that decorated the wall, swirling and threatening to take everything away. The letter, the glow she saw in her parents' room, the strange man, the way her mom was acting, the strange but familiar boy in her dreams, and the mystery girl. Effie didn't understand what was happening.

The way her mother acted is what disturbed Effie the most. She had never seen her mother that way before. Her mother was always honest. Effie never had reason to suspect that she would hide anything. Of course, there were the white lies that *all* parents told their children. She remembered when she was very little, maybe three or four, she saw a dead squirrel in the park. Effie asked what was wrong with the squirrel and her mother told her it was just sleeping: 'taking a nap.' Effie knew at the time it didn't seem quite right, but her mother's answer still made her feel relieved. That kind of lie a child could always expect from their parents. It would probably be the same lies that Effie would say one day when she became a parent. But this was much different and it made Effie feel different about her mother — made her feel something towards her she had never felt before and Effie didn't like the feeling.

The glow in her parents' room was something different entirely. Effie remembered times where her imagination seemed so real she couldn't tell the difference between what was real and what was not. But that sort of thing hadn't happened to her since she was much younger. Why was it happening now?

Effie wasn't sure about her mystery girl, but she felt she was somehow important to everything that was happening. Effie needed to find out who she was. Maybe it would also help her find out the identity of the mystery man. Effie felt as though the two were somehow connected. A knock on the door broke her concentration.

"Hey sleepy head, are you coming to breakfast?"

Effie got out of her bunk. She opened the blinds to see the sun being enveloped by threatening clouds. As Effie dressed, she looked at the framed pictures of art projects she and her brother had made throughout the years. Her mother always framed her favorite art project Jimmy and Effie had made over the summer. She smiled at the progression she could see in the pictures as their skill grew with age. Effie emerged from her room to find the family sitting around the table: Jimmy, buried in a book, Liz clearing the table, and Michael agitated at not knowing how the day would be filled.

Effie stood and stared at her family. It was how every day started, but this one didn't feel the same.

"What's wrong, Honey? Not hungry? Not feeling well?"

Liz put her hand on Effie's forehead. Her soft hands smelled like flowers from the dish detergent. Effie shrunk from her mother's touch.

"I'm fine!" Effie snapped.

Effie's response made Liz more suspicious. It raised Jimmy and Michael's attention as well. They both stopped what they were doing to stare at Effie. Effie felt her face redden with all her family's eyes looking at her. To her relief, the phone rang. The chime of the bells broke the awkward silence. Liz answered the phone. Effie saw Jimmy shoot her a look as if to tell her to stop acting weird.

"Hello? Oh, hi, Lydia. Hmmm, I'm not sure if she's up to it..."

"What is it?!" Effie interrupted.

Liz stopped. Her face contorted with concern brought on by Effie's continued change in behavior.

"Well sweetie, Larry and Jodi need to go to the shop and Lydia's at home babysitting Andrew. Since it looks like it will be a rainy day, she wondered if you wanted to help her sit."

"Sure!" Effie said in a completely new tone.

"Well, you show me you can eat your breakfast…"

"Can I go, too?" Jimmy asked as Effie began to eat her pancakes as fast as she could.

Liz paused.

"Yes!" everyone could hear Lydia reply on the lime-colored phone receiver.

Effie and Jimmy left the house. Jimmy turned to Effie. She wanted to tell her brother about the mystery girl and her nightmares. Still, Effie worried that Jimmy's world of logic and evidence would just drive the wedge between them further.

"I'm going to the library to do some research," Jimmy said.

"Research?"

Jimmy sighed and looked at Effie.

"Seriously Eff, weren't you listening the other night? The adults were telling us all about how Crystal Beach used to bring people in with boats?"

Effie looked at Jimmy blankly.

"I was thinking the library might also have some old school yearbooks. Maybe we could find the name you saw there. Maybe the letter was from when Mom and that man went to school together."

They arrived at Derby Road, which led to the Davies' street. Jimmy kept walking along Erie Road towards the library.

Effie turned up Derby Road, leaving the sounds of the amusement park behind her. She looked at the storefronts that lined Derby approaching Queen's Circle. Effie usually loved the colorful storefronts, but today was different. Her mood was clouded by everything that was happening.

Effie turned on Belfast Road South. The pastel houses grew larger to accommodate year-round living. Effie walked up to Lydia's house. She opened the door before Effie could knock then peered around.

"Where's Jimmy?"

"Off being a detective."

Lydia nodded, "Come in!"

The warm wood floors and the bright-colored walls filled with family pictures felt welcoming. The house always smelled of food, in a good way, like a restaurant. It wasn't musty like the cottage. As soon as she entered, Spinz jumped up to lick her face.

"Spinz!" Lydia chided and pulled her dog off Effie.

Effie wiped her wet face and bent down to give Spinz a pet, his tail wagging. Effie noticed Lydia staring at the bag she brought.

"Oh, I brought some things…"

"Music?"

Effie nodded. Lydia grabbed her friend's arm enthusiastically.

"Let's go to my room!"

"Where's Sniff?"

"If it's quiet, I don't ask questions."

The two sat in Lydia's room, which was covered in posters. Prince, George Michael, and David Bowie all looked at Effie with sultry eyes. The pink walls were barely visible behind the posters and Bristol board. Polaroid pictures filled the colorful Bristol board surface. Effie liked to stare at Lydia's pictures full of her and her friends' silly faces, fashion poses, and laughter. Effie thought that they were a window to her future, and it looked like a fun and happy one.

Effie emptied the contents of her bag on Lydia's ballerina bed sheets. Bright orange bangles, a mixed tape and some rock band pins spilled out. Lydia looked down at the treasure. She took the tape and put it in her small white bedside cassette player and pressed play. Madonna's

Borderline blared out. Lydia jumped up and began to dance on her bed, bouncing to the music. Effie smiled, staring.

"Don't just stand there!"

Lydia pulled Effie onto the bed.

A loud click-clack was heard from the hall outside Lydia's room. The two paused.

"Is that your mom?"

Lydia looked confused. She turned off the music.

"Mom?"

The click-clack got louder and more hurried. Effie felt her chest tighten as the expression on her friend's face twisted from concern to worry.

Sniff broke through the door, giving them both a start, followed by Spinz. He was wearing his mother's leopard-skin patterned high-heeled shoes and had his hands on his hips.

"Now they won't say I'm too short for the pirate ride!"

Lydia and Effie looked at Sniff, then at each other and erupted in laughter.

"What? Pirates have peg legs!" Sniff appealed.

Lydia turned on the music again and pulled Sniff onto the bed while Spinz barked and ran in circles.

After they had danced themselves out, Lydia and Effie flopped onto her bed. Sniff disappeared, leaving the leopard skin heels behind.

"You're so lucky," Effie told Lydia.

Lydia looked confused.

"What do you mean?"

"You get to live *here* all year. I bet it's the best."

Lydia frowned.

"What's wrong?"

"Well, of course it feels that way to you Eff. This is your *vacation*. You get to go home to the big city. I always thought *you* were the lucky one."

Effie looked around. Her eyes rested on the pictures on her wall. "But it looks like so much fun."

"Yeah, those are the fun times," Lydia smiled, "but things aren't easy around here. Dad says Crystal Beach is dying."

"How could that be? It's so perfect here!"

"I don't know. Dad says they closed some factories in Port Colborne and that fewer and fewer people are coming to the park. I know it's true. A lot of the people in those pictures moved away. The classrooms are a little emptier every year."

Effie frowned as she looked at the pictures.

As she looked among the faces, a thought came to her. The green-eyed girl! Maybe she was in the pictures! Maybe Lydia knew her! Effie's eyes darted from Polaroid to Polaroid, but her mystery girl was nowhere to be found.

"Do you know a green-eyed girl? She kind of has wavy hair. She's a little older than you, I think," Effie asked, still looking at the photos.

"No, I don't know a green-eyed girl. If she were still here, I'd know her. Everyone knows everyone in Crystal Beach."

After a long pause, Effie glanced back at Lydia.

"Dad says we may have to move, too. He said business isn't as good anymore. We may have to close the store."

"Oh no!" Effie didn't know what to say. She rushed beside her friend. "Is it for sure?"

Lydia shook her head.

"I don't know."

Effie could feel Lydia's emotions wash over her and couldn't help the tears from welling up in her eyes. Effie wanted to say something helpful, but didn't know the right words to say.

They heard the downstairs door open and the two could hear Lydia's parents arrive home.

"Lydia? Sniff?" Jodi called out.

Lydia composed herself and forced herself to brighten.

"Here, Mom! Effie's here too!"

She held her friend's hand and smiled.

"C'mon, let's be happy." Effie returned the smile.

The two made their way downstairs. Larry was busy unloading the car. Jodi welcomed the girls with a warm smile.

"Effie, Lydia!" She paused and asked suspiciously, "Where's Sniff?"

"Playing dress-up, I think." Lydia failed to mention that the *dress-up* was happening in her parents' closet.

"Sit down, sit down. Let me get you something to eat!"

The girls sat down. Jodi made them some sandwiches. The hazelnut gooiness oozed out from between the slices of bread. Jodi asked lots of questions of the girls. She liked the 'girl talk.' Jodi kept sneaking glances at Effie. When Lydia left for the washroom and they were alone, Jodi leaned in close.

"What's wrong, honey?"

Effie shrugged. She didn't want to tell her secret.

"What do you mean?" Effie said unconvincingly.

Jodi smiled and put her hand on Effie's.

"Honey, I can see something is wrong. It's plain to see in your aura."

Effie felt tears begin to well in her eyes. She didn't want to cry in front of Jodi, but there was a part of her that did.

Jodi could see Effie's internal struggle. She caressed Effie's hand.

"Sometimes, the secrets we keep can be our undoing. It may not be time to tell, but when it's time, don't stay closed."

Effie began to cry. Jodi hugged her close.

"Don't worry, Effie. I'm sure it will pass. Trust your parents. They can help."

"What if *they're* the problem?"

"Is it what you *see* that's the problem or what you *feel* is the problem?"

"What I've seen."

Jodi paused thoughtfully and smiled at Effie. "What you think you see may not be what it seems. Trust your heart."

When it was time to leave, Effie gave Jodi and Lydia a big hug and started her walk back to the cottage. The sun had come out once again. The dampness from the afternoon rain gave the air a thick fragrance. Maybe it was the rain, but Crystal Beach looked different. It wasn't as bright and colorful as she remembered. Effie noticed a new detail. Every other house had long blanched grass. There were beer cans and bottles on some lawns, and many house exteriors had peeling paint and rotting wood. Many of the stores she passed on the way from the Davies' house had *for lease* or *for rent* signs in the windows.

***

Effie entered her cottage wondering if her brother Jimmy had found anything at the library. As Effie entered the living room, she saw her mother sitting on the tweed brown couch. As she approached her mother, Effie heard a sob.

"Mom?"

Elizabeth stiffened and turned towards her daughter. Tears were streaming down her face.

"Mom, what's wrong?"

Effie rushed to her mother. As Effie got close, she noticed that Elizabeth had a photo album on her lap. Elizabeth smiled and closed the photo album.

"Nothing, Honey," Elizabeth replied as she gathered Effie into her arms.

"Just remembering some happy times."

"Aren't times happy now?"

"Oh yes, the *happiest!*"

Elizabeth kissed the top of Effie's head. She rose and put the album back in the bookcase. Effie was careful to take notice. She needed to share everything with her brother.

"Is Jimmy home?"

"No, Honey, not yet." Elizabeth paused.

"Wait, wasn't he with you?"

Effie panicked. She forgot.

"Um, yeah, but he stopped to talk to some boys in the park so we got separated."

Effie's response seemed to satisfy Elizabeth.

"Did you have fun babysitting at the Davies'?"

Effie nodded.

"Good, come help me with dinner. I'm sure we need something extra healthy to make up for whatever you ate there."

Effie got up and joined her mother in the kitchen, glancing back at the photo album on the bookcase.

Chapter 9
The Investigation Continues

Dinner was quiet. Michael dragged Jimmy home from the library after Effie confessed. Effie didn't want to tell, but, as it got dark, Effie's original story didn't hold up, especially under her parents' questioning.

"Who was he with at the park? It's after dinner. I want to call their parents."

When worry turned to panic, Effie confessed before her parents called the police to assemble a search party.

Jimmy pushed the food around his plate. He wore a disappointed look on his face. Effie wasn't sure if it was because he didn't find anything at the library, or if it was because he was scolded. Effie felt bad but whether or not Jimmy had any news, *she* had news that she needed to share.

Jimmy and Effie snuck to their room as quickly as they could without arousing suspicion. When Effie was sure it was safe to talk, she blurted out, "Well?"

Jimmy sighed, "Nothing. No yearbooks."

"What about the boats?"

"They stopped long before Mom was old enough to get a letter. They stopped before she could read. The only thing that happened with a boat around the right time was some girl drowning."

He paused and climbed into the top bunk.

"Mom and Dad were married about twelve years ago. They met a few years earlier at university. The timeline just doesn't work."

Effie pondered. She wanted to tell her brother everything she had been going through. But she had been holding back because she was worried. Worried that the wedge between them would grow. Effie sighed. Then a thought filled her mind. Maybe the wedge was there because she wasn't sharing! Maybe all she needed to do was tell Jimmy everything.

"Jimmy?" Effie climbed into her bed. It was easier to confess to the upper bunk than to Jimmy's face. *It* wouldn't scrutinize her if her plan backfired.

"Yeah?" Effie heard Jimmy reply from behind the wooden board.

"I've been seeing things," Effie confessed.

All was silent. Effie heard Jimmy move in his bed, then his face appeared from over the bunk.

"What do you mean?"

Effie told Jimmy about the night she was searching for the letter, the whispers, the light. Everything spilled out of her. Effie kept talking, afraid Jimmy would interrupt with his skepticism and cold, detective-like interrogation. Jimmy just stared at Effie. His look was suspicious, just as Effie had feared.

"You don't believe me!?"

Jimmy shook his head then disappeared. Effie heard a thump as he lay back in his bed.

"What's wrong?" Effie asked, but she knew the answer. Now the cold wooden plank seemed less comforting. She was wrong. The wedge had just grown bigger.

"Ever heard of a wild goose chase?" Jimmy replied.

"Of course, I have! What has it got to do with anything?"

"Jeez, Eff, a letter that only you've seen? Seeing things that couldn't possibly happen? It feels like you've sent us on a wild goose chase."

Jimmy paused.

"Have you told Mom or Dad?"

Effie shook her head. She couldn't speak. She was too mad at her brother. She was mad at herself for taking a risk. Effie felt her face redden. She didn't want to cry. She felt it would make her even less believable to her brother. She felt it would make her seem broken.

"I think you should Eff. What if it's something serious? Something from your accid…"

"I saw Mom crying when I got home today!" Effie defended herself. She knew something was happening. It needed to be figured out. She wasn't crazy.

"What?!" The upper bunk creaked as Jimmy's head reappeared.

"She was crying looking at a photo album"

"Are you sure?"

Effie nodded.

"Did you see the picture?"

Effie shook her head. She could see the suspicious look return.

"I saw where she put it," Effie added quickly.

Jimmy's expression didn't change.

"I didn't see the picture, but I think I could figure out *which* page the picture was on."

"You sure?"

Effie nodded.

Jimmy jumped out of bed. Effie watched as he crept to the door and opened it quietly. He peeked out and turned back to Effie.

"They're in their room," Jimmy said in a whisper.

Effie just stared.

"C'mon!" Jimmy waved her towards him.

Effie crept out of bed. Her heart began to race. She tip-toed to her brother who stood watch at the door. Effie joined him. Jimmy opened it wider so Effie could peer out.

"Where is it?" he whispered.

Effie pointed to the pine bookcase. It seemed miles away. Their "cozy" cottage never felt so big.

Jimmy crept out of the room. Effie clutched his shirt and followed closely behind.

As they crossed the living room, Effie's head began to throb. She was overwhelmed with a mix of fear and nerves. As they approached the bookcase, the rustle of whispers returned. They started behind her parents' door but quickly swirled around her. Effie peered around, trying to understand what was happening. Jimmy shook her from her daze.

"What's wrong with you?" he whispered angrily.

"What?"

Effie hadn't realized they had stopped. They were in front of the bookcase. The whispers scattered and silence returned.

"Which one is it? How many times do I have to ask?"

Effie's eyes came into focus. She found the photo album and pointed. Jimmy took it off of the shelf and shoved it in her chest. Effie felt like they weren't on the same team. This was her chance to prove to him she wasn't broken.

"Show me!" Jimmy's whispers were getting louder.

"Okay!" Effie's whispers weren't any quieter.

"Shhhhhhh!" Jimmy hushed even louder.

Effie flipped through the photo album. She found the page she was looking for and stopped. She was shocked. The photo album fell from her hands and landed on the floor with a loud thump. The album fell open to the page she was looking at. It was empty. The photos were gone!

"What are you doing?" Jimmy whispered and looked at their parents' bedroom door.

Effie looked at her brother.

"They're gone!?"

Their parents' bedroom door burst open. Michael lurched forward. He was draped in bed sheets and waved a wooden clothes hanger as a weapon. He tripped and fell to the floor with a loud thud. The sheets engulfed him completely.

Jimmy and Effie could hear a muffled, "Who's there?! You better run! I've called the police and I'm a black-belt

Karate master!" Michael lied as he thrashed to free himself. His head popped out from underneath the sheets, his arms still trying to escape.

"What are you two doing? You scared us to death!" Jimmy and Effie could hear Elizabeth call from the doorway.

Jimmy and Effie helped free their father while they desperately looked at each other for a good answer to their mother's question.

"Um, we were hungry for a snack, but it was dark and I bumped into the bookcase…" Jimmy began.

"Snack!" Michael's head emerged from the mess of sheets. "That sounds like a great idea!"

Chapter 10
The Third Dream

Effie's heart felt full. It was a feeling she had never felt before. She liked it. It was a bright summer day. The sunshine washed over her. Her emotions swelled inside her. She felt as if she was going to burst.

A smile stretched wide across her face. Her polka-dot dress danced playfully in the warm summer breeze.

She knew she was waiting for something, but what?

Effie felt someone's hands wrap around her waist. Her heart leapt. Effie spun around, face to face with a camera. She jumped in surprise. The camera clicked and spit out a photo. Behind the camera was a boy. *The boy*, the one she had seen in her other dreams. He smiled. The camera stared at Effie with a picture hanging out of it like a tongue.

Effie snatched the photo and looked at it.

"Hey!" the boy said. "That's mine!"

"Not if it's a picture of me!"

Effie looked at the picture. It was pale white.

"It's blank?"

"You have to shake it."

Effie stared at the picture. She didn't understand.

"Here. Let me show you." The boy took the picture from Effie. He started to wave it in the air like a fan. He looked ridiculous. Effie couldn't help but laugh.

"What?" the boy smiled.

"Nothing," Effie lied. She could tell the boy knew.

"I love your laugh," the boy confessed. He quickly moved the camera to his face and began taking pictures.

"Wait, what are you doing?" Effie laughed and began to run. But she wasn't trying to get away. As they ran in circles, the boy continued to take pictures. Effie giggled as she watched him shake the pictures. He tried to hold on to the handful of photos he had collected, but as he waved his latest photo they all burst into the air.

As the pictures fell to the ground, Effie went to help pick them up. She picked up a picture and looked at it. It wasn't of her. It was a picture of the girl she had been seeing around town.

"This isn't me."

"What do you mean? These are all of you."

He started handing over the pictures. Effie began to rifle through them. They were all of the girl she had seen around town. They weren't of her running or laughing on a sunny day. They were taken in different places, with different people.

In one, the girl was crying. The other, she was yelling at an older man. There was one where she was running away, afraid at night. In the last one, she was pale, her hair fanned in the air. She was surrounded by darkness, eyes wide staring back. She dropped the picture to the ground.

"What's wrong?"

"This can't be right." Effie rifled through the pictures. She found a picture of the boy crying while looking at pictures. Another was of an older man and woman. They wore black and were very sad.

The boy reached out, sensing Effie was becoming increasingly worried. He touched her shoulder.

Just then, a man yelled. Effie recognized the voice, even though she had never heard it before. She looked up at the boy. He was afraid. She was afraid. The voice yelled a name, what was it? It wasn't Effie. The voice yelled the name again. Effie knew he was yelling at her, but she didn't know the name. The voice got closer. It was angry, furious. Effie was too afraid to look back. She looked into the boy's face.

"Run," was all she could say.

The boy sprang to his feet. He collected as many pictures as he could carry, and then ran.

Effie felt a firm grip on her shoulder. It hurt. Effie woke up.

Chapter 11
Effie's Gift Revealed and the Collision

Jimmy walked in silence. After Effie couldn't produce the picture she had seen her mother crying over, the day had been awkward between Jimmy and Effie. The friends walked aimlessly throughout Crystal Beach in thoughtful silence. Effie felt defeated. She didn't know how she could make Jimmy believe her. Lydia sensed the tension and complied with their silence.

Something from above interrupted the awkward quiet. An acorn hit Jimmy on the side of his head. Jimmy clutched his ear and yelped.

"Ow!"

The friends stopped. At first, Effie didn't know what had happened. She saw Jimmy looking at an acorn on the ground. The confused friends looked up at the trees. Another acorn hit Effie's shoulder. The friends realized that the acorns weren't coming from above. They were coming from behind. They all turned as another acorn hit Jimmy in the chest. They saw Mertz laughing, getting ready to throw another one.

"Mertz! Stop being such a jerk!" Lydia yelled.

Mertz dropped the acorns and walked towards the friends. Effie's heart was beating fast. Whenever Mertz was around it put Effie on edge. But her heart wasn't beating out of fear. Effie was furious. Her mouth was dry. As Mertz approached, Effie began to hear the familiar rustling. It got louder as he got closer.

Mertz began to say something but the rustling overtook Effie. She couldn't hear anything Mertz was saying. It sucked her in like a vortex and washed over her. The rustle turned into whispers, but the words were unintelligible. Effie saw Lydia talking back to Mertz. She was obviously mad but Effie couldn't hear a word she was yelling.

As the whispers became clear, Effie could hear they were words. Then, like a wave, Effie realized what the whispers were revealing to her: secrets about Mertz, things she shouldn't know.

Mertz pointed threateningly at Jimmy's chest. Lydia tried to push him away, but it wasn't working. Effie's head was throbbing, she was an observer behind a wall of whispers. Effie saw Mertz clench his fists. She could feel what he was thinking. She could feel he was going to hit Jimmy. It was at that moment that Effie found her voice.

"Get out of here, Mertz!"

Everyone froze and looked at Effie.

"It isn't our fault that we don't live here. Your dad is wrong! We're not the problem. We love it here. It isn't our fault he lost his job! Maybe he's a jerk like you and no one wants him around!"

"Effie!" Lydia was shocked.

But Effie couldn't stop. The voices in her head urged her to keep talking.

"It's not *our* fault your mother doesn't live with you anymore! Maybe it *is* your fault! Maybe she left because you're as much of a jerk as your dad!"

Effie stopped. She knew she went too far. There was complete silence. Mertz stared at Effie. His mouth was open in shock. Effie could feel Mertz's feelings change. His anger was still there but something else started to seep in. Mertz's face reddened. She could see his eyes well up with tears. His lips began to quiver. His fists clenched harder. Lydia may not have been able to feel Mertz's emotions like Effie but she could see what was happening.

"RUN!" Lydia yelled.

Jimmy, Effie, and Lydia all ran. Mertz stood in shock, rooted to the sidewalk. The friends could hear him wail threats after them.

"What was that?" asked Jimmy.

"It was the whispers. They told me."

"How did you know those things?" Lydia huffed.

"I don't know. I just sort of hear..." but Effie wasn't able to finish her sentence. As soon as the friends turned up Queen's Circle, they crashed into a man. There was a collective "oomph" as they collided. The bags the man was carrying crashed to the ground along with the friends.

"Oh no!" the man exclaimed. He was more worried about what he had dropped than anything else.

"We're sorry!" Lydia quickly explained. They bent down to help.

"Don't!" the man yelled. The friends all stopped and stared at the man. Jimmy and Effie recognized him as the man they saw with their mother on the pier.

"Sorry to snap, it's just there could be broken glass. I don't want you to cut yourself," the man explained. He looked in each bag.

"Phew! Nothing broken," the man paused. "You kids gotta be more careful!" His voice quickly changed from relief to annoyance.

Effie and Jimmy were too surprised to speak. They nodded.

"We know. We're really sorry."

The man surveyed the kids and his face warmed.

"Remember to skate with your head up!" he said in a friendlier tone. He smiled. Effie recognized the smile. It was familiar but she didn't know why.

The friends helped him collect his bags. He thanked them and continued along Queen's Circle. When he was out of ear shot, the twins turned to each other and said in unison, "It's him!"

Lydia looked at them. "Who?"

"It's the man we saw with our mom on the pier the other day," Effie explained.

Lydia looked at them both. She didn't know what to say.

"We have to follow him!" Effie exclaimed.

"Are you sure it's him?" Lydia asked.

The twins nodded. The friends checked over their shoulder. Satisfied that Mertz wasn't on their tail, they rushed to catch up to the man. As he came into view, Jimmy waved them back.

"Slow down, we don't want him to notice!"

They watched the man enter a shop. *Crystal Memories Photo and Framing.*

"What now?" Effie asked.

"We wait," Jimmy said, not taking his eyes off the store.

Lydia sighed. Effie could tell it wasn't Lydia's idea of a fun afternoon. In the silence, Effie noticed Lydia's face twist.

It was the kind of face one makes when they're hit with a pillow and didn't see it coming.

"Um, Effie?"

"Yes?"

"How did you know all that stuff about Mertz?"

Effie paused. She felt her face flush. She didn't want to keep secrets from her friend. Everything that had been happening to her poured out. Lydia listened intently and Effie could tell she believed her. Effie was relieved. She was nervous that Lydia would not believe her, just like Jimmy didn't. But Effie noticed that Jimmy didn't seem to be reacting the way she expected. He seemed supportive, not skeptical. He nodded. He was listening and agreeing with her. Effie's heart leapt.

"But how did this happen? When did it start?"

"I don't know? It just started…"

"The accident." Jimmy interrupted his sister. Effie slouched. Everything was about the accident. She worried there was nothing she could do to change that. Jimmy noticed Effie's withdrawal and continued.

"They said seeing and hearing things could be an after-effect. Who knew those *after-affects* would tell you things."

"But it doesn't make sense!" Effie exclaimed.

Jimmy shrugged. "Sherlock Holmes says that if you eliminate all other possibilities, then whatever is left, even if it's unbelievable, must be true. Right now, it's the only explanation that makes sense."

There was a pause. The non-believer was converted. But he still thought of Effie as *'changed'*.

"What now?" Effie asked.

"We wait and we watch. Hopefully, this man will lead us to the answers." Jimmy said resolutely. Effie was agitated. She didn't want to wait. She wanted answers *now*. Effie jumped up and rushed towards the store.

"Where are you going?" Jimmy called.

"Don't worry, I'll be quick."

Effie came out of the store as quickly as she went in. There was a bounce to her step, one that signaled a successful mission. Effie held a card in her hand and showed it to Lydia and Jimmy.

The card read:

Crystal Memories Photos and Framing

Owner: Harvey Wallace

Photography, Framing, and Camera
Sales and Service since 1970

"That's the name!" Effie told her friends.

Jimmy frowned.

"Are you sure?"

Effie nodded. Lydia was confused.

"From the *letter*," Effie explained.

Lydia looked at her two friends. "Okay, what now?"

"We investigate," Jimmy replied.

Chapter 12
Liz Fails the Test

Lydia and Effie walked together, alone. Jimmy had walked ahead, muttering to himself. His mind was busy assembling the evidence.

"Did you already know the stuff about Mertz?" Effie asked Lydia. But she somehow already knew the answer.

Lydia nodded, "Eugene tells me everything."

Effie paused. She looked at Lydia. She started to feel her sadness.

"Is Eugene your boyfriend?"

Lydia smiled, but the tears that welled up in her eyes couldn't hide how she felt. She shrugged.

"Not if he moves away."

Effie felt horrible for her friend. She wanted to console her. Effie could feel how Lydia felt, but she had no idea what to say to make her friend feel better. When they reached Jimmy and Effie's house, Effie turned to her friend. She hugged her close. It was the first time Effie had hugged someone that way. It wasn't a hug to console a scraped knee. It was a hug to help heal a much deeper wound. One that a band-aid couldn't fix. She felt Lydia hug back. She was holding Effie as if she were clinging to hope: a hope that

the things she feared would not come to pass. Lydia lifted her face and smiled at Effie. It was a smile that showed a new appreciation of her friend: that their difference in age no longer separated them. Before Lydia left, Jimmy asked her to find out all she could about Harvey Wallace from her parents.

Jimmy and Effie entered their cottage to find they were alone. Jimmy's shoulders slouched. Getting closer to the truth would have to wait. Noticing her brother's dejection, Effie was struck by an idea. She couldn't contain her excitement.

"Perfect!"

"What do you mean?" Jimmy asked.

"You wanted evidence."

Jimmy nodded.

"Well, just follow my lead. Hurry!"

Effie pulled Jimmy into their parents' bedroom.

"I'll look for the letter. You put this card on the kitchen table."

Effie handed Jimmy the card she had collected from Harvey Wallace's store.

"Why?"

"You'll see, just let me know if Mom and Dad come home."

Jimmy disappeared into the kitchen and left Effie alone.

Effie began to look for the letter. She could feel her heart begin to race. The other night came rushing back to her. The thump of her heart spread to her head. Whispers danced around the room and brushed her ear. A loud thump scattered the whispers. She was about to rush out of the room, thinking the thump signaled the return of her parents, but before she could leave, the thump happened again. Effie realized the thump had come from inside the bedroom. The thumping began to quicken, as if it were in a panic. Effie's eyes raced around the room.

"Hurry!" Jimmy called from the kitchen.

Effie couldn't move. The panicked thumping increased and got more intense. The letter was the last thing on her mind.

"C'mon, I hear the car." Jimmy rushed into the bedroom and grabbed Effie's arm. He pulled her into the living room.

Effie awoke from her daze. "I'll go to our room and watch through the door. You say I'm napping."

Jimmy looked at his sister. He was confused.

"Grab a book and watch Mom from the couch."

Effie rushed into their bedroom and shut the door. The thumping was gone. She stood alone in silence, left to ponder what had happened. Effie peeked out of the bedroom. She watched Jimmy run around the kitchen table, then find a spot on the couch with a book. Jimmy shifted and looked back at the table. Once he was satisfied, he opened the book and began to read.

Liz entered the cottage.

"Kids?!"

"Here, Mom!" Jimmy called back. "Effie's taking a nap."

"Nap?"

"She had a headache." Jimmy quickly lied.

Liz nodded. This was a common occurrence since the accident. She walked into the kitchen and put her purse on the table.

"Well, your fath..."

Liz paused as she noticed the card on the table. She picked it up and looked around suspiciously. She looked at Jimmy. Satisfied that he was buried in a book, she slipped the card quickly into her purse, checking to see if Michael had come in from the car. Effie could see Jimmy was watching. It was the evidence he needed. He folded the book shut and made his way to the kitchen.

"Did you see the card on the table? A man came to the…"

"Shhhh!" Liz hushed. She looked back at the door. "He came to the door? That's…" Liz began to mutter to herself.

"Who is he?" Jimmy asked.

"Hush! Your dad's coming. He can't know."

"Why n…"

"Shhhh!"

Michael walked in, carrying groceries from the car.

"We have dinner!" he said triumphantly.

"Jimmy, help your dad with the groceries."

"Me, need help? Hah, I don't think so!" Michael boasted, showing his strength by lifting the bags of groceries above his head. As soon as the bags were over Michael's head, they burst open, spilling all over him and onto the ground.

"Aw…" Michael began, but before he could finish the sentence, Liz interrupted with a sharp, "Jimmy. Help your father!"

Jimmy rushed to collect what had fallen. His father bent down to help, looking up, smiling.

"Tonight, they're doing fireworks at the park!"

"I'm not sure Effie will be up to it," Liz called to Michael from the kitchen. "She's having a nap. Jimmy said she had a headache."

Effie opened the door and joined her family.

"I'm fine, Mom. I just needed a little rest."

"Then, it's settled! I'll make some hot dogs and we'll go to the park. We're going to meet the Davies!"

Jimmy glanced at Effie with a look that said, *did you see?* Effie nodded at her brother. She could feel their connection. The wedge was lifting.

Effie looked at her mother who had regained her composure and began busying herself in the kitchen. She frowned at her dad who had his arms full of loose groceries. As he made his way to the kitchen, the loose items slipped and fell. In an effort to catch some before they hit the ground, Michael promptly hit his head on the counter.

"Ow!"

Effie ran to his side to help.

"Thanks, Hon," Michael leaned and kissed Effie on the top of her head.

"I love the park at night," he said with a smile.

Effie looked up at her father and smiled back. "The place looks magical with all the lights! And the fireworks are awesome!" He continued. After placing the groceries on the counter with her father, Effie felt his arm on her shoulder. "I'm glad you're feeling better, Hon," Michael said with a tender smile.

"And, I'm sorry."

"For what?" Effie asked.

Michael stroked her hair and said, "I think you may have a little of me in you, which may have…" Effie felt the rush of feelings and thoughts from her father. She had realized that it had always been that way since the accident. The whispers would tell her things, about people, about what they felt, about what they feared. Effie could feel that her father blamed himself for her accident. She met his watery gaze with a warm smile.

"It was just an accident, Dad."

He smiled again. Effie's reassurance made the moisture in his eyes quiver.

"How about some hot dogs? I'm starving."

"Now you're talking!" Michael said, and Effie could feel her father return to his usual self as he grabbed a package of hot dogs and made his way to the barbeque.

Chapter 13
Confrontation in the Park

Effie felt the swell of excitement all around her, as though she was floating. The emotion of the park engulfed her.

The spell was broken when her brother dug his fingers into her arm.

"I need you to focus."

"Huh?"

"Don't space out."

Effie nodded. She knew her brother was counting on her. The larger crowd and darkness would make it more difficult. Effie felt a large hand clap her back. Jimmy must have felt the same as he let out a big breath.

"Effie! Sherlock! Where are those hippie parents of yours?"

They turned to see Larry. His broad face smiled back at them. Jodi was pulling Sniff along behind him. Lydia rushed to meet her friends. Larry quickly noticed Michael and Liz and made his way to greet them. Jimmy had to find out how Lydia had done on her assignment.

"Well, did you find out anything about Harvey?"

Lydia looked around her and spoke quickly in a low voice.

"Mom said they knew Harvey from high school. She said he was a sad man, something about him losing love and never being the same again."

"What does that mean?" Jimmy scowled.

Lydia shrugged.

"I tried to find out more but…"

"Arrrrrrrrrrrrrrrrrrrrrr!" Sniff interrupted.

"But *that* happened." Lydia glanced over to her brother.

"Who's going to take me to me pirate rides?!" Sniff half-asked/half-demanded as he pulled on his sister's arm towards the heart of the park.

The parents noticed the kids pull away. Adults always lingered to speak. They never seemed to be able to do more than one thing at a time. They called after the friends.

"You guys stay together. We're going for a walk on the pier."

The parents started off towards the pier. Jimmy nodded after them. "Let's follow!" He yelled so he could be heard above the noise of the crowd.

Luckily for Lydia's arm, the pier was in the same direction that Sniff was pulling. The friends walked into the center of the amusement park. Sniff couldn't hide his disappointment when he found the Jolly Roger ride was still closed, but it didn't last long. The Pirate ride caught his attention and changed his mood for the better.

The pirate ship cut through the air, leaving a trail of light behind it. As the friends approached the Pirate, the parents made their way to the pier. Jimmy found a spot near the ride where he could keep an eye on them. Effie watched, too, but couldn't help being overwhelmed by the laughter and excitement that surrounded them. The Galaxy, Flying Chairs, Tilt-A-Whirl, and Flying Bobs enclosed them. Effie's senses were flooded from the gleaming lights, laughter from ride-goers, excited chatter and loud music. She watched Jimmy. He was a statue surrounded by a sea of movement, completely focused. She watched Lydia at the Pirate. Eugene was working the ride. Effie saw Lydia flick her hair and noticed a change in her body language as she leaned into Eugene. Eugene smiled broadly as his face flushed. Sniff was jumping up and down gleefully. Lydia's connection had opened the door for Sniff's dream of pirate adventure to come true.

"I've lost them!" Jimmy interrupted Effie's trance.

"What?"

"Mom and Dad, I've lost them on the pier, c'mon!"

Jimmy grabbed Effie's arm and pulled. They ran towards the pier. As they plunged into the crowd, Effie felt as though she was travelling through time. The people seemed to age before Effie's eyes. From kids and teenagers to adults walking arm in arm, to grandparents sneaking away for some quiet, hoping the calmness of Lake Erie would provide an escape from the commotion. The noise faded behind them as Jimmy and Effie searched for their parents.

"Where did they go?" Jimmy said exasperated.

Effie looked around, but she couldn't recognize anyone in the sea of faces. She shrugged, signaling to her brother that she wasn't having any luck either.

"Remember what I told you about Sherlock Holmes?" Jimmy asked his sister.

"Something about evidence?"

"No, that when you eliminate the impossible, whatever you're left with, no matter how crazy, must be the truth."

"Okay?"

"Well, I'm going to ask you something I would've thought sounded crazy a few days ago. Can you *feel* them?"

"What do you mean?" Effie asked.

"Don't make me explain. I hate even asking it. *You know*, it's about whatever you've been able to do lately?"

Pirate
Photo: William E. Kae

Sky Ride
Photo: Rudy Wolowiec

"I don't know?"

"Try! See if you can."

Effie looked around. She was anxious. Jimmy, picking up on her sister's nerves, put his hand on her shoulder.

"Calm down and concentrate."

Effie closed her eyes. She took deep breaths. She felt her heart slow and she became calm. She felt Jimmy's support. His belief in her. It gave her strength. The jumble of whispers started to separate. When Effie opened her eyes, she could pick out the threads of whispers like strings from a cat's cradle. Effie looked down to the beach where the waves crashed against the shoreline. People walked along the damp sand barefoot. She could feel things and hear whispers coming from the people on the beach. They were too faint to make out, but all of them were unfamiliar. Behind her, the illuminated Comet roller coaster rumbled against the blue-black sky, still darkening from the sunset. Effie turned to see if she could feel or hear anything. Aside from the teenage excitement, there was nothing familiar. Overhead, people sat side-by-side on the Sky Ride. The emotions and whispers that rained down on Effie were of both budding and mature romances. What she heard and felt made her smile, but again, nothing struck her as familiar. Effie turned to her brother and shook her head.

"Maybe they went back to the games." Jimmy thought aloud.

Effie nodded at the possibility and they both plunged back into the heart of the park to see if they could find their parents. The Penny Arcade was aglow. Its neon lights beckoned park-goers to enter. It was like a lighthouse among a sea of people. The sidewalk was lit up with hot pink and green; the aisles of games were strung with lights. Outrageously-dressed workers shouted at passersby, attempting to goad them into a try.

"You work your way up the games. I'll check the Arcade." Jimmy pointed in the direction that he wanted Effie to start the search.

"Effie!"

Effie heard her name called and turned around to see Lydia walking with a downtrodden Sniff.

"Why did you guys leave? I couldn't find you."

"We lost our parents. We're trying to find them," Effie explained to her friend. As she spoke, the familiar sound of whispers came to her from the end of the games.

"What's wrong with Sniff?" Effie asked, doing her best to focus.

"Oh, he puked on the pirate ride."

"I guess I'm just a landlubber," Sniff said in a saddened voice, his pirate twang completely gone.

The whispers began to get louder. Effie looked up the aisle of games. They seemed to be coming from where the new Ferris Wheel was located.

"Effie! You're supposed to be looking for Mom!" Jimmy called coming around the corner from the neon-lit Penny Arcade.

"*Sorry*, Lydia just found us with Sniff."

Jimmy stood staring at her with crossed arms.

"Okay, I'll go!" Effie huffed. She turned to follow the whispers that beckoned to her. Just then, a familiar "Oh Yeah!" rang out.

Mertz emerged from the Midway crowd. He immediately moved towards Jimmy. Jimmy didn't take his eyes off of Effie. She could feel him urging her to go and look for their mom and not to worry about him. Then she saw her. Effie's mystery girl stood against the moving crowd. She was soaked head to toe. She stared at Effie as people passed her as if she were invisible. The girl's stare warmed to a smile. She giggled and bounced off. The whispering became louder. It surrounded her. Effie's head began to throb. She couldn't hear anything but the whispers. She was being sucked in like a whirlpool, the strange girl at the center. Her surroundings fell away and she followed. As she moved closer to what she thought was the center of the sound, she heard her name.

"*Effie, Effie!*"

Effie turned to the voice. It was still coming from somewhere beyond the Ferris Wheel. Effie checked back on her brother and friends. She could see Lydia and Mertz yelling at each other. Jimmy's eyes were still fixed on Effie. Her head throbbed. She felt like she was watching from a different world, behind a window. She was being pulled further away.

"Effie!"

Effie followed the voice. The gentle turn of the Ferris Wheel seemed out of place with the bustle of the park. The circular motion felt like it was the center of the vortex, pulling Effie in. The mystery girl stood and stared and then ran off towards the bright red of the Laff in the Dark ride. Effie's dream from the other night hadn't helped how she felt about the ride.

"Effie!"

The voice called again but it wasn't the voice she had expected. It was familiar but not the same as the laugh or whisper she had heard from the mystery girl. Effie also realized the voice wasn't coming from the Ferris Wheel. As she approached, she saw Charmin' Charles, the piano-playing skeleton in a long dark gown, turn to her.

"Effie, why haven't you visited us?" Charles said to her, his jawbone chattering and hollow eyes staring through her.

Charmin' Charles
Photo: Rudy Wolowiec

Effie looked around. Her head throbbed and now her heart raced. No one in the crowd seemed to notice.

"Sam and Sal have something they want to tell you." Charles hissed and raised his bony arm, pointing his sharp fingers towards the heart of the ride.

Effie moved along in silence. As she approached the front of the ride, she saw Laffin' Sam and Sal. Their broad smiles and squinting eyes made them appear as menacing as ever. Effie wanted to run, but she was paralyzed. She couldn't escape. She knew her only hope was to keep going.

As Effie approached, both Sam and Sal lost their plastic smiles and looked at her directly. Sal, in her outrageous dress and oversized hat, and Sam, in his loud, checkered pants and mismatched vest and tie, stared at Effie as she approached.

The three stood in silence. Effie's heart and head pounded. The movement and sound that surrounded her had melted away. Everything was drowned out by the silence that seemed to engulf Effie.

"She's confused," Sam said to Sal. Sal nodded. The flower on top of her hat quivered.

"She doesn't understand, Dear," Sal said to Sam. Effie could only stare. She was frozen in fear.

"It's your gift, Effie. What you see isn't always there, Hon," Sal said to Effie. Effie opened her mouth to speak, but the words didn't come.

Sam shook his head and frowned. His ginger hair shook.

"It may not be there, but what she's able to see with her gift is always true," Sam said to his partner, his freckled rosy cheeks expanding and contracting as his mouth moved.

"Yes Dear, you'll need to learn to tell the difference between what is real and what is true," Sal explained to Effie.

"She'll need to learn how to use what she sees to get to the truth," Sam said to Sal.

"What's happening to me?!" the words erupted from Effie.

The two stopped their conversation. They frowned and looked at Effie. Sal was the first to speak.

"Didn't you hear me? It's your gift, Hon."

"I don't understand!?" The crowd continued swirling around, seemingly unaware of Effie and her heated exchange with Sal and Sam. Effie realized that Sal and Sam were in her head. They could hear her thoughts.

"Go to your mother. It will become clear," Sam replied.

"Where is she?!"

"The Scrambler," Sal and Sam said in unison. And everything stopped. The vortex broke away. She was

Laughin' Sal
Photo: Rudy Wolowiec

released. The park noise returned with a rush that flooded her senses.

"*Go!*" Effie heard a whisper in her ear and she broke into a run.

Effie ran back to the games as quickly as she could to get her brother. As she approached, she saw Mertz grabbing Jimmy. One hand clenched a handful of Jimmy's shirt. Lydia was yelling at Mertz, who was keeping Lydia and Sniff at bay with his free arm.

As Effie approached, Jimmy turned and spotted her.

"She's at the Scrambler!" Effie yelled to Jimmy.

After hearing her call, Jimmy, in one swift motion, grabbed Mertz's arm and twisted. Mertz was taken by surprise. Jimmy had a hold of Mertz's hand. He thrust his leg behind Mertz, who fell to the ground with a loud thump.

"Ooomph!" Mertz exhaled. Lydia and Sniff both jumped back in surprise.

Jimmy didn't let go of Mertz's hand. He applied pressure and Mertz howled.

"OOOOOOOOOOWWWWWWWWWWWWWWWW! Let go! Let go!"

Tears welled in Mertz's eyes. Jimmy released his hold and ran to join his sister. Lydia and Sniff followed.

"Wow Jimmy, where did you learn to do that?!" Sniff asked Jimmy running beside him.

"A book: *The Ancient Arts of Karate and its Secrets Revealed*," Jimmy responded without breaking his stride.

As the friends approached the Scrambler, its lit tentacles spun, thrilling the riders who raised their arms and yelled with excitement. Effie noticed her mom talking to Harvey in front of the ride. Effie pointed to let Jimmy know she had spotted her, but Jimmy already knew. Harvey was giving Liz a gift, an ornately wrapped package with a silk blue ribbon.

"Mom!" Jimmy yelled. Liz was startled. She looked around and spotted her children. Effie could see her mother's eyes searching to see if they were alone. It was obvious she didn't want to be spotted by Michael.

"Kids? What?" but Liz wasn't able to get over her surprise before Jimmy began interrogating her.

"Who is this? How do you know him? Why is he giving you a gift? Are you breaking up with Dad?"

Liz, completely surprised by the questions, stammered. "What? No? Why would you think that?"

Effie, caught up in the excitement, grabbed the gift and began tearing at the paper.

"Effie!" Liz yelled.

As Effie pulled away the paper, she found a framed picture. It must have been the one Liz was looking at in their cottage, Effie thought. Also in the frame was a letter. Liz grabbed it back.

"What do you think you two are doing?" Liz was furious. Harvey stared helplessly, not knowing what to do. Lydia and Sniff were also frozen. Some passersby began to stare.

"Liz?" Michael called as he approached with a concerned look on his face. Larry and Jodi were with him.

"Why did you sneak away?" Michael asked.

"Oh, it's all ruined!" Liz cried. Michael moved quickly to console her.

"What's ruined, Honey?"

"Everything? You've found out!"

"Found out what?"

While Michael was consoling Liz, Effie looked closer at the framed picture.

"That Mom's been secretly meeting with this man!" Jimmy said pointing.

"What?!?" the adults said in unison.

During the commotion, Effie looked over the picture frame. The letter looked different. It was her father's handwriting and signed with his name.

"It isn't the same letter!" Effie exclaimed.

"What?" Michael said, taking the frame from Effie. He looked it over.

"Hey, this is the first poem I wrote for you," Michael said to Liz. His eyes looked back to the frame. "And, this is the photo we took on our first date at the park." Larry came up behind him and stared over Michael's shoulder.

"Hey, I took that picture!" Larry exclaimed, slapping Michael on the back. Michael fumbled the picture frame to a collective gasp. He secured it to everyone's relief.

"It was supposed to be a surprise!" Liz sobbed. "For our anniversary!"

"Oh, Honey, it's perfect!" Michael said, hugging Liz as the picture frame slipped out of his hands and crashed to the ground, shattering.

Everyone froze and looked at the damage.

"Don't worry, I'll replace it! Free of charge," Harvey said.

Chapter 14
The Fourth Dream

After the amusement park fiasco, Jimmy and Effie had spent most of the evening with their heads bowed in shame as they faced a barrage of questions from their parents. But both Jimmy and Effie remained silent. There weren't any words that could explain why they had acted the way they did. They both knew if they told the *truth* it would stir up concern in their parents and it would likely land Effie back in the city seeing specialist after specialist or worse, the hospital. Effie and Jimmy went to bed. Effie couldn't help but notice Jimmy shooting angry looks in her direction. She understood that he wasn't happy with her. He hated being wrong and, worse than that, that he "fell" for her stories. After a long silence in their bunks, Effie found the courage to ask her brother.

"Do you believe me about the letter? There is a different one! That's not the one I saw."

Jimmy was silent. Effie wasn't sure if he was thinking or giving her the silent treatment.

"I wasn't making it up!" Effie pleaded.

She heard Jimmy take a long sigh.

"I believe *that*."

"What does that mean?"

"I believe that *you believe* what you told me. And because you believed it, I believed you."

"I still don't understand."

"Just because you believe it happened doesn't actually mean it happened, Eff."

"You think I'm lying?"

"That's not what I'm worried about."

"You're worried?"

"Eff, you had an accident, you see things and hear things, things that aren't possible for other people to hear. Yes, I'm worried."

"But you said you have to believe it if everything else is… is… whatever that Sherlock says." Effie was feeling the tears stream down her face.

"Yeah I know, but you were wrong Eff. So it's different."

"But it happened!" Effie needed her brother to believe her.

"Okay, but why didn't we tell Mom or Dad?"

"*They* wouldn't believe us. I'd just have to go have more tests."

"You're right, which is what I'm worried about, too."

"I don't want to have more tests. I don't like the hospital."

"I know. I don't want you to go through that either."

Effie sighed.

"I need to sleep, Eff. I just need to figure everything out."

"Don't tell Mom and Dad."

"I won't, not yet."

Effie heard Jimmy yawn.

"Goodnight." She said.

Jimmy grunted and Effie heard him shift in his bed. The wedge between them had returned. Effie's exhaustion overtook her racing thoughts and pulled her into the depths of sleep.

When Effie opened her eyes she was looking down at her blue polka-dot dress. The boy was holding her outstretched arms and frowning. They were covered with bruises.

"Run away with me," he pleaded.

"I can't. He'll find us and do worse!" Effie was crying.

"You don't have to stay. Come with me, I'll protect you."

Effie looked at the frail boy. She knew he couldn't protect her. She knew that *he* might hurt the boy if *he* found out. Effie knew she didn't want anything bad to happen to the boy.

"I don't think we should see each other anymore."

Effie could see the surprise in the boy's face. His eyes welled. The boy shook his head and began to fade away. Effie reached out to grab him but found her hand going into a tangle of branches. She was standing outside the cottage. The sun washed over her. Her heart raced. She looked up and down the street. The colors of the cottages were brighter, as if they had all been given a new coat of paint. Effie had something in her hand. A note. She unfolded it, reading the words:

"Meet me at the pier tonight."

Effie recognized the writing. She had seen it before. Her heart filled with excitement. She glanced around, knowing that she'd be in danger if she were discovered. Effie rushed into the cottage. It looked very different on the inside. There was no wallpaper. It was covered in faux wood panels. Effie glanced around, nervous. She raced into her parents' bedroom. Their room was also very different. White wall panels and pink accents decorated the room. Effie knew where she was going. She moved a dresser. Behind was a loose panel. She opened it. Behind the panel was a pile of papers and pictures. She stuffed the note inside. Effie heard the door open and a man's voice bellow. She could feel her fear overtake her. She knew she didn't want to be caught by the man that owned the voice or there would be more bruises.

***

The cool night air rushed into her lungs. Effie was running. She was excited but afraid. She was doing something she shouldn't. She could see the pier. She was almost there. Then she heard *his* bellow. *He* was looking for her. It was her stepfather and he was angry. Effie knew she couldn't let him find her, or worse, find her with the boy. Effie ran to the dock. She was alone. She heard the voice of her stepfather get closer. Effie spotted a boat beside the pier. The boat swayed on the dark water. Effie checked over her shoulder. She knew it wouldn't be long before her stepfather would spot her. She had nowhere to go. Effie looked at the wobbly boat as it rose and fell with the tide. She stepped in the boat. The boat rose and fell. Effie felt unsteady with one foot on the pier and the other in the unsteady vessel. She heard another call. Effie's head rose and looked into the darkness. It was her stepfather, but his voice was distant. He was headed away from the pier! Effie gave a sigh of relief. She would find the boy and tell him everything. Maybe he could help. Maybe the police would help. Maybe she could stay and start a new life with someone she cared for and knew cared for her.

Effie relaxed. The tension washed away. She knew what she was going to do. As she pulled her leg from the boat, Effie lost her balance. Before she knew it, the boat tipped and Effie was submerged. She struggled to get above water but was trapped under the boat. She tried to grab hold but her hands slipped. She felt the weight of the water begin to pull her down. She panicked. The hollow boat echoed as her hands failed to grasp anything and slipped back into the water. It was the same thump Effie had heard in her parents' bedroom. The weight of her arms started to burn. Her dress became heavier from the weight of the water, which seemed to grab a hold of her and pull her into its depths. Effie saw the night sky ripple as she slid underwater and into darkness.

Chapter 15
Doubt then Light

Effie awoke with a gasp. She heard a clap of thunder and rain beat against the window. She looked around. Her room was dark. The door of the room opened and a rush of sound swirled around her.

"Get out of my head!" Effie said aloud and then quickly closed her mouth. She heard Jimmy shift in his bunk. Effie paused. He was still asleep.

The whispers got louder. Effie tried to ignore them. She concentrated on replaying everything from the day. There was a piece missing. She needed to put it together. What did Jodi say? What did Sal and Sam say?

"Your head can trick you."

"What you've seen is true "

"Real and true can be different."

"It's my gift."

The whispers got louder. They were almost yelling in Effie's ear. A streak of lightning illuminated her room. What was happening to her *was* real. She was sure of it. The whispers filled her head, making it feel like it was about to explode. Effie tried to fight off the strain but it was too much. She put her hands on her head, trying to contain the pressure. Then amidst the swirl of sound, Effie heard the distinct voices of Sal and Sam. Their voices rang through the jumble.

This was her gift.

What if she tried to just listen and stop fighting?

Effie was afraid. She didn't know what would happen if she let the whispers take over. She felt like she would drown in them. But it was too much for her to fight. It was the only thing she could do. She had to listen to them and stop fighting. As Effie opened her heart to her gift, the rush of voices made everything clear. She wasn't broken. She was improved .

Effie sat up in bed. She knew what she had to do. It was all because of the stepfather. She hated him. She hated him for *her*, for the mystery girl. It was because of him she was bruised. It was her fear of him that prevented her from telling the boy how she felt because she didn't want him to get hurt too. It was because of her fear of him that she died. She knew the truth. Effie would show her family. They would know she isn't broken.

Effie hopped out of her bunk. Her bare feet touched down lightly on the floor. She checked back to be sure that Jimmy wasn't awake. The whispers were gone. Effie could hear the rain wash against the window and the distant rumble of thunder. She listened. She could hear Jimmy's deep breathing. Her feet peeled off the plastic linoleum floor. Effie made her way to the kitchen, fumbling in the darkness. She was lost. The whispers returned. They guided her where she needed to go. Effie grabbed long scissors from the counter. The rain had stopped. The bright moon emerging from behind a cloud sent light all over the counter. From the gleam of the scissors' sharp metal, Effie could see a reflection. It wasn't her. It was the mystery girl staring back at her. Effie wasn't scared. This was who had been whispering to her all along. Effie smiled at the pretty girl. She smiled back. Her eyes twinkled jade green. Effie wanted to help free her. She needed Effie's help.

Effie crept into her parents' room. Light shone from behind the bed. It was the glow she had seen all along. As she approached, she heard her father.

"Huh? J? Eff? Is that you?"

Effie was silent, focused completely on what she had to do.

Michael got up.

"Effie? What are you doing?"

As she approached the foot of the bed she could see light coming from behind the wall.

"Effie, what are you holding?" Effie could hear her father's voice. He was fully alert and she could hear the worry in his voice.

Effie didn't respond. She kept moving towards the light. Her family needed to know she wasn't broken. The light became a starburst that pulled her in.

"Effie!" Michael said loudly. The tone and volume of his voice woke up Liz.

"What's going on?" Liz said sleepily.

Michael was getting out of bed.

"It's Effie! She has something in her hand!"

Liz woke up instantly and shot up out of bed. Her head swiveled, trying to make out where Effie was. Michael was out of bed rushing to Effie but he was too far. It was too late.

Effie was completely blinded by the light, but she knew what she had to do. She could hear her parents, her mother yelling, her father rushing to her. Soon they would all understand her gift. She knew Jimmy was awake and would be there soon. But none of them could stop her now.

Effie plunged the scissors blindly into the center of the light like the voices asked her to do. It was what the girl needed. She needed Effie to free her. Free her from her stepfather and all the secrets. The scissors split the dark wallpaper. They slid in easily. The wallpaper was covering something hollow. Effie felt the scissors stop and hit something hard. She pulled the scissors away, tearing the wallpaper open. The light, the noise, everything stopped. Everything was normal. Well, almost normal. Liz was yelling at her. Michael had reached her, grabbed her shoulders and had begun shaking her. He must have thought she was sleepwalking. Jimmy stood at the door, worried. Effie was the only one who was calm and knew exactly what was going on.

"Dad!" Effie yelled.

Michael stopped shaking her. He stared at her blankly. Effie looked past him to the wall. Michael turned his head. A secret compartment was behind the torn wallpaper. Inside was a pile of letters and pictures.

Chapter 16
The Explanation(s)

The room was silent. All eyes were on the secret compartment. Michael slowly turned and pulled out the letter and pictures. He glanced over the letter and then started to shuffle through the pictures.

As Michael was concentrating on the pictures, Effie grabbed the letter. Michael was too focused to notice. Effie glanced over the letter. It was the same one she had seen on their first day in Crystal Beach. Jimmy slid beside her and whispered in her ear.

"Is that the letter?"

Effie nodded. Liz had gotten out of bed and joined Michael.

"It's Harvey!" Liz exclaimed.

"I knew I recognized him. Wow, this must be from twenty years ago. I don't know who *she* is."

Liz's face scrunched into a squint.

"Wait. I think I remember her. Poor girl, her face was in the papers. She drowned one summer. It was tragic."

Each family member took turns looking at the pictures. When Liz read the letter she burst into tears.

"It's *sooo* romantic!"

Michael took the letter from Liz.

"Oh, Liz you're always so dramatic. Let *me* see."

As he read the letter, his eyes welled up with tears.

"They were so in love!" he stammered, tears streaming down his face.

The excitement of the discovery didn't last long. Effie had to explain herself. Jimmy helped as best as he could. Both didn't want to say anything about Effie's new abilities. So together they wove a story. Jimmy explained he found out who owned their cottage when he was researching at the library. This wasn't exactly true. Effie told her parents Lydia's story about Harvey's lost love. She also explained that she noticed a soft spot on the wall when she was playing with Sniff. These were all white lies. Like the ones parents tell to protect their children. These lies were to protect the parents. Effie said she must have been sleepwalking the whole time in her parents' bedroom because she didn't remember a thing. This was a plain lie.

Liz and Michael watched them intently and listened closely to everything they said. After the kids' story, they looked at each other, muttered something about the 'sub-conscious' and seemed satisfied. Adults always had a way of explaining things away. It was *their gift* Effie thought to herself.

Epilogue

The next morning was quiet. Effie thumbed through the pictures. She squinted at the images of Harvey. He looked much different. The girl on the other hand, with her curly hair and sparkling green eyes, was the same girl she had been seeing since they arrived. She *was* Effie's destiny and Effie was happy she could help her. Harvey and the girl seemed very happy in the pictures. Effie remembered how she felt when she *was* the girl and knew she had cared for Harvey very much. The girl was Harvey's lost love Lydia's parents had mentioned.

All the while, Jimmy was, of course, buried in a book, occasionally shooting Effie a suspicious look.

Michael brought in breakfast. He paused noticing Jimmy's book, "Hey buddy, what's with the book? Run out of things to read?"

Effie looked at the book cover for the first time. *ESP, Psychics and Other Paranormal Phenomenon*

Jimmy put down the book and shrugged.

"No, just wanted something different," he replied, matter-of-factly, but his eyes were on Effie as if to say: *I'm going to figure out the mystery of you.* The wedge was gone. Jimmy was no longer worried about Effie being fragile. Effie was happy, because she wanted someone to help her unravel her new gift. She didn't want to do it alone. She was excited about her and Jimmy being close again.

Michael shrugged.

"Well c'mon. You gotta eat." The late morning sun was bright. As the twins sat down to eat, the doorbell rang. They could hear Liz answer.

"Um, hi Sniff – " Liz tried not to giggle.

"Andrew!" The twins could hear Sniff reply with a sophisticated air. Everyone at the table stopped.

"Sorry, *Andrew*, we're all sit…"

Everyone in the family interrupted Liz. They all had to see Sniff's change first hand.

Andrew stood at the door. The pirate shirt was gone. It was replaced with a tuxedo shirt. The change in wardrobe wasn't what made Liz giggle. And Liz wasn't the only one covering her mouth trying to contain laughter. Andrew was also wearing Groucho Marx black plastic glasses attached to a big rubber nose and fake moustache. Michael didn't react fast enough and laughed heartily, quickly covering his mouth.

"Sni… Andrew, I'm sorry, Hon. What are you supposed to be?"

"A bookworm, of course," Andrew responded matter-of-factly, trying to maintain a look of sophistication. He saw Jimmy and immediately asked.

"Do you have that Karate book I can read?"

Jimmy smiled, "I didn't bring it, but maybe later we'll go to the library."

Later in the day, the family dropped off the letter and pictures to Harvey at his store. He seemed very happy to get them and couldn't stop thanking Jimmy and Effie. He was so grateful that he had sent a gift basket to their cottage.

"Finally, something for me! This is the best gift ever!" Michael said triumphantly, getting his hands on the gift basket full of the treats that had eluded him since they arrived.

"Ahem," Liz interrupted, reminding Michael of the anniversary gift he had just received.

"The second best gift ever!" Michael quickly corrected.

The turbulent events that threatened the stability of their family were behind them. A calm washed over the family and carried them back to the familiar vacation that Effie was so fond of. The whispering and headaches had stopped. Laffin' Sal, Sam, and Charmin' Charles didn't speak to Effie again, though she did visit them several times. Her fear of the Laff in the Dark ride was also behind her.

Eugene began to hang around the friends or at least hang around Lydia while she was with Jimmy and Effie. More Eugene meant more Mertz. But whether it was Eugene's presence or what happened the night at the amusement park, Mertz seemed to want to become friends, especially with Jimmy. On the drive home, Crystal Beach looked very different to Effie. Effie noticed many of the cute cottages seemed aged and decayed. She noticed the unkempt yards, the graffiti on the closed storefronts, and that many of the shops seemed abandoned. Effie knew that her favorite place in the world hadn't changed during their vacation. She knew that the change was in her.

The End

Λcknowledgements

When a book is published, it's often only the author's name that is printed. This doesn't reflect the numerous people that contributed to the finished product that finds its way into the reader's hand. I would be remiss if I didn't take some time to acknowledge those that made Mystic possible.

Much of the credit goes to my first audience. My children. Nathan and Miranda, who provided the reactions I needed to help guide where to take the story. My partner Sarah, who continues to be a source of inspiration and encouragement to turn my ideas into something tangible. June and Bob, who always patiently survive the painful iterations of my writing until it comes into form. Dawn Matheson, who helped make Mystic presentable to publishers with her editing prowess. The wonderful support of William E. Kae, who was always approachable and donated his personal time and photos to help Mystic capture the essence of Crystal Beach. It's beyond unfortunate that William was unable to read the finished work that he contributed to as he passed in September of 2020. The incredibly supportive friends of Crystal Beach, who answered the call for photo donations. Rudy Wolowiec and Sue and Rudy Bonifacio. Shane Artbuthnott, who read early iterations of Mystic and provided such wonderful advice to help mold Effie into a strong protagonist. Jeremy Luke Hill of Vocamus Press, who is such a great supporter of the literary arts and local writers. And of course, the team at Histria Kids: Kurt Brackob, Dana Ungureanu, Diana Livesay, and their team for helping to create an amazing cover as well as being so supportive of Mystic; taking a chance on the story so it could get in the hands of readers around the world.

HISTRIA

BOOKS

FOR OTHER GREAT TITLES FOR CHILDREN
AND YOUNG ADULTS, VISIT

HISTRIABOOKS.COM